CAR18

D1101955

70003872719X

Six are they, the Badgers' Crowns

If power ye seek, they must be found

Crystal, iron and flaming fire

Gather them, if ye desire

Ice, and wood and carven stone

The power they give

Is yours

Alone

SUNDERED LANDS

FULL CIRCLE

BY ALLAN FREWIN JONES
AND GARY CHALK

ILLUSTRATIONS BY

GARY
CHALK

Hodder
Children's
Books

A division of Hachette Children's Books

Text and illustrations copyright © 2011
Allan Frewin Jones and Gary Chalk

First published in Great Britain in 2011
by Hodder Children's Books

The right of Allan Frewin Jones and Gary Chalk to be identified as the
Authors of this Work has been asserted by them in accordance with the
Copyright, Designs and Patents Act 1988.

1

All rights reserved. Apart from any use permitted under UK copyright
law, this publication may only be reproduced, stored or transmitted, in
any form, or by any means, with prior permission in writing from the
publishers or in the case of reprographic production in accordance with
the terms of licenses issued by the Copyright Licensing Agency and may
not be otherwise circulated in any form of binding or cover other than
that in which it is published and without a similar condition being
imposed on the subsequent purchaser.

All characters in this publication are fictitious and any resemblance to
real persons, living or dead, is purely coincidental.

A Catalogue record for this book is available from the British Library

ISBN 978 0 340 98814 5

Typeset by Avon DataSet Ltd, Bidford on Avon, Warwickshire
Printed and bound by CPI Group (UK) Ltd, Croydon, CR0 4YY

The paper and board used in this paperback by Hodder Children's Books
are natural recyclable products made from wood grown in sustainable
forests. The manufacturing processes conform to the environmental
regulations of the country of origin.

Hodder Children's Books
A division of Hachette Children's Books
338 Euston Road, London NW1 3BH
An Hachette UK company
www.hachette.co.uk

The Sundered Lands Chronicles:

Trundle's Quest

Fair Wind to Widdershins

Fire Over Swallowhaven

The Ice Gate of Spyre

Sargasso Skies

Full Circle

Visit **www.sunderedlands.co.uk** for sneak peeks,
games, competitions and prizes

Prologue

The legends say that once, long, long ago, there was a single round world, like a ball floating in space, and that it was ruled over by six wise badgers. The legends also tell of a tremendous explosion, an explosion so huge that it shattered the round world into a thousand fragments, a vast archipelago of islands adrift in the sky. As time passed, the survivors of the explosion thrived and prospered and gave their scattered island homes a name – and that name was the Sundered Lands.

That's what the legends say.

But who believes in legends nowadays?

Well . . . Esmeralda Lightfoot, the Princess in Darkness, does, for one. According to Esmeralda, the truth of the ancient legends was revealed to her in a reading of the Magical and Ancient Badger Blocks – a set of prophetic wooden tokens from the Old Times. And reluctant hero Trundle Boldoak believes it as well, and between them they have already found five of the six crowns that the prophecy said they must seek.

But there is a problem. Someone else is also hunting for the Six Crowns – his name is Captain Grizzletusk, and he's the meanest, bloodthirstiest, wickedest pirate ever to sail the skies of the Sundered Lands. And just to make matters even worse, Grizzletusk and his murderous pirate band are being helped by none other than Millie Rose Thorne, Queen of all the Roamanys, and – horrifyingly enough – Esmeralda's very own aunty!

They have outdistanced their enemies for the

time being, and have arrived at the Guild of

Observators in the crumbling old city of Widdershins,

seeking help from the Herald Persuivant . . . Percy, to

his friends . . .

1

Return to
Widdershins

'Trundle! Duck!'

Esmeralda's warning came only just in time.
Trundle flung himself to the floor as a huge leather-
bound book came swooping towards him, wide open
and with its pages crackling and flapping.

He covered his head with both paws as the
thrashing pages of the book grazed past him. The book

rose again and sailed on, rebounding off an oak-panelled wall and cartwheeling up towards the ornate ceiling.

And the book wasn't the only missile flying around the room. Not by a long way. Inkpots whistled to and fro, papers and parchments and documents rose in fountains and fell in blizzards. Scrolls whisked this way and that like great, trapped insects with wings of red tape. And adding to the chaos and the confusion were paperweights and letter openers and candlesticks and pens. Not to mention dozens of albums and textbooks and encyclopaedias that flocked around the room like great ungainly birds.

Peering out from between his fingers, Trundle saw Esmeralda dive behind the Herald Persuivant's leather sofa as a volley of quills zipped past her like arrows and embedded themselves in the wall.

And in another part of the room, the Herald

Persuivant himself, their dear friend Percy, was wielding a walking stick, batting away blotters and inkpads and sticks of sealing wax.

'We have to get the crowns apart!' Percy yelled as he gave a candlesnuffer a wallop that sent it spinning through the air. 'It's the only way to stop this!'

It was the crowns that were causing all the trouble.

Little did Trundle guess as he and Esmeralda moored *The Thief in the Night* to a crumbling pillar in a quiet, uninhabited quarter of the College of the Guild of Observators that their visit would be the cause of such a riot!

Keeping out of sight, and with three of the crowns in their arms, they had made their way to Percy's private office, slipping into cover every time a badger strode past with his trail of book-laden minions. Several times they dived into the shadows when a troop of fox guards had come stumping along the corridors with their clanking armour and their rusty weapons.

Finally they had reached the Herald Persuivant's door. He had been delighted to see them – and even more delighted when they showed him the three crowns they had brought with them. The Crown of Fire, in its old biscuit tin, the Crown of Ice safe and sound in the container the Lamas of Spyre had made, and last but not least, the Crown of Wood in its box with *Five of Six* engraved on the lid and with the final clue pasted within.

Percy had closed and locked his door behind his visitors. Then he had cleared space on his desk, and the three crowns had been taken out of their boxes and placed reverently on the dark mahogany surface.

'You've done marvellously well, my friends,' he told them, slowly circling the desk and examining the crowns from every angle.

Esmeralda beamed with pride. 'It wasn't easy, I can tell you that!' she said. 'The phoenix wasn't at all like you might have thought – he was old and grouchy and scraggy – and we were in a battle – and we met up with a pirate hare who was completely out of his gourd!'

'He ended up as an Oracle in a monastery,' added Trundle. 'And that's a whole other story!'

'My, my,' said Percy. 'I see you've had quite the adventure!'

'More than one adventure, Percy,' said Esmeralda. 'We haven't even told you about the lizards and the flying Opera House and the steammoles! And Jack is now principal rebec player in an orchestra that's touring all the outer islands of the Sundered Lands to packed houses.'

'Well, I never!' Percy straightened up and smiled at them. 'And to think, that after all these hundreds and hundreds of years, two little people like you should track down five of the six ancient crowns!' He laughed. 'Extraordinary!'

'I think I like *that* one best,' said Trundle, gazing at the Crown of Fire, sitting atop its biscuit tin. Its long, cool, slender flames flickered and fluttered like ribbons in a breeze. Trundle thought it was probably the most beautiful and fascinating thing he had ever seen.

'I still prefer the Crystal Crown,' said

Esmeralda. 'Because that's the one that started it all off.' She looked at Percy. 'You still have the first two crowns safe, don't you?'

'Indeed I do,' Percy said.

'Could you get them out?' asked Trundle. 'I'd love to see all five together!'

'An excellent notion!' Percy said. 'Wait here a moment, while I go and fetch them.'

He returned a little while later with the Crowns of Crystal and Iron, which he placed with the others on the desk.

'Outstanding!' Esmeralda breathed, gazing at the crowns in wonder.

'Extraordinary!' Percy murmured.

'I'll say!' a spellbound Trundle agreed. Gathered together like that, the five crowns made a spectacular and breathtaking sight.

But they hadn't been given much time for

standing and staring. The first thing that had alerted them to the trouble that was coming was a faint, raspy humming sound like a distant swarm of angry wasps.

'What's that noise?' Esmeralda had asked. 'And why is it getting louder?'

But before anyone had the opportunity to respond, the source of the humming became all too clear. The crowns had started to vibrate, gently at first, but gradually more and more agitatedly. And as they quivered and shook, so they had moved towards each other across the desk.

'Oh, dear,' Percy had said. 'I don't like the look of that. Perhaps we should—'

And it had been at that precise moment that the whole room had gone crazy.

'We have to get the crowns apart! It's the only way to stop this!'

That's easier said than done, Percy! thought Trundle as a wooden in-tray flashed past the tip of his snout and crashed into the wall with a loud bang.

Keeping low to the floorboards, he crawled towards the desk. The heavy piece of furniture was shaking and rocking, its legs drumming on the floor like impatient fingers.

From the corner of his eye, he saw that Esmeralda was also advancing slowly on the desk, using a huge atlas as a shield against the flying objects.

He reached the desk and gradually lifted himself so he could peer over the top. The five crowns were in a ring, whirling round and round so quickly that they were just a bewildering blur in front of his eyes.

'Do something!' howled Esmeralda. 'Stop them, Trun!'

Trundle drew his sword and with a thundering heart and screwed-up eyes he poked the blade into the furiously spinning tempest, hoping to slow the whizzing crowns down enough for them to be pulled apart.

'Ow!' There was a clang and a crash and the sword was knocked out of his grip. 'Ow! Ow! Ow!' he yelped, hopping from foot to foot and wringing his stinging paw.

But it had done the trick. The five crowns went careering in all directions around the room, bouncing off the walls and the ceiling and the floor, hissing and spitting like meteors.

Esmeralda fended off the Crown of Wood with her atlas. It crashed to the boards at her feet and she leaped forward on to it, dropping the book and grabbing the crown in both arms.

At more or less the same moment, Percy made a flying leap for a cupboard door, flinging it open just as the Crown of Fire zipped past him. The crown shot

straight into the cupboard and Percy slammed the door on it.

'Trundle! Stop messing about and get one of the crowns!' hollered Esmeralda, as the Crown of Wood heaved and bucked under her, struggling to get free.

Blowing one final time on his tingling fingers, Trundle gave a mighty pounce, and more by luck than judgement, he managed to snatch the Crown of Iron out of the air.

He ran to a wall-cabinet, whipped the door open and bowled the crown inside. The precious object clanged and rang as he whisked the door shut behind it.

The effect was immediate. Everything that had been flying and careering through the air suddenly came crashing and bashing and whacking and cracking to the floor.

Percy picked up the Crown of Ice, popped it back into its container and shoved it into a drawer in his desk. Then he found the Crown of Crystal and put it on a high shelf. An exhausted silence filled the room.

Esmeralda got to her feet, the peaceful and immobile Crown of Wood in her paws. 'Let's . . . *not* . . . do that . . . again . . .' she panted.

'I had no idea they would react like that!' gasped Percy.

Trundle gazed around the wreckage-strewn room. 'If this is what happens when *five* of them meet – what will it be like if all six of them are put together?'

'That's a very good question, Trundle, my friend,' said Percy, stooping to pick up a few scattered things and put them back on the desk.

Trundle and Esmeralda joined him in tidying up as best they could.

'And do you have a very good *answer* to that very good question, Percy?' Esmeralda asked. 'I mean, some of the old legends say that when the crowns come together, the Sundered Lands will be reunited – that all the islands will join up again into one big world. But other stories just say that a huge source of unimaginable power will be released. So, which is it, do you think?'

Percy pursed his lips. 'Well, now,' he said thoughtfully. 'I suppose it could be one . . . or the other . . . or both. After all, it would take a huge amount of power to pull all the islands of the Sundered Lands back together again, wouldn't it?' He rubbed his hands, palm to palm. 'It could be just like the old legends say – or it could be something quite different and unexpected!' His eyes gleamed excitedly. 'Who knows? After all these long years of waiting, there might be a big surprise in store for everyone!'

'But you're sure it's . . . *safe* . . . to put them together?' Trundle asked dubiously.

'Safe?' murmured Percy. 'Oh, well, I couldn't promise it'll be *safe* exactly.' He laughed softly. 'But that's no reason for giving up, Trundle, my friend. No reason at all!'

'No one's talking about giving up, Percy,' said Esmeralda. 'In fact, we plan on doing the exact opposite of giving up, don't we, Trun?'

'Um . . . yes . . .' agreed Trundle. 'Absolutely.' He retrieved his sword from a corner of the room and slipped it into his belt.

'Which is why we came here,' added Esmeralda, picking up the box that had housed the Crown of Wood and planting it on the desk in front of Percy. 'Are you any good with riddles, Perce?' she asked. 'Can you tell us what this clue means?'

Percy leaned in close over the open box,

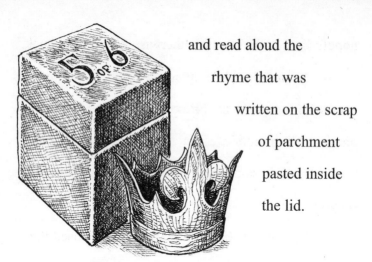 and read aloud the
rhyme that was
written on the scrap
of parchment
pasted inside
the lid.

Ye players of the ancient game
Who plot y'r course with might and main
Shall all the crowns unite again
Among the stones of Trembling Plain

Then ye who would the Badgers' cause abet
Fly swift and true towards Sunsett.

'Hmmm,' said Percy, rubbing his chin and looking
worried.

'Do you know what it means?' Trundle asked

hopefully. 'I hope you do, otherwise we're a bit stuck.'

'Hmmm,' said Percy again. He began to pace up and down the room, his brow furrowed and his chin in his paw. 'Hmmmm.'

'Percy?' said Esmeralda. 'We're really counting on you.'

Percy strode back to the desk and perused the rhyme once more. 'Well, I can certainly explain Sunsett to you,' he said. 'Although if I'm right, it's most definitely not good news. Not at all, it isn't.'

'Go for it, Percy,' said Esmeralda. 'Tell us the worst!'

'Well, my friends, Sunsett is the name of the land where the ancient Badger Lords lived before the world was broken into fragments.' He peered from Esmeralda to Trundle. 'And if the quest can only be fulfilled by flying to Sunsett, then I'm afraid the quest will never be fulfilled.' He sighed, his shoulders slumping under his sky blue robes.

'I've spent my whole life helping to map all the islands of the Sundered Lands,' he murmured. 'And I can tell you without a shadow of a doubt – there is no such place any more as Sunsett.' He dropped back into his chair as if all the life had drained out of him. 'Sunsett must have been blown to bits in the explosion,' he groaned. 'The whole quest has been a complete waste of time!'

The Orrery Chamber

Trundle stared in dismay at the Herald Persuivant.
Their friend suddenly looked very old and careworn as
he slumped miserably in his chair. *Poor Percy*, Trundle
thought, *I didn't realize our quest meant so much to
him*. And the normally unquenchable Esmeralda was
also speechless for once, rooted to the spot, goggling at
Percy with her mouth hanging open.

'Sunsett was blown to bits?' gasped Trundle. 'Are you sure?'

Percy glared crossly at him. 'I said so, didn't I?' he growled.

'Yes, but, look here,' stammered Trundle. 'I mean, seriously, that can't be right.'

'A waste of time . . .' murmured Esmeralda gloomily. '. . . a complete waste of time . . .'

'No!' Trundle declared. 'No! No! And furthermore, *no*!' He frowned at Esmeralda. 'I simply won't believe that the Fates would bring us all this way and then just abandon us like that.' He gave her an encouraging smile. 'Come on, Es – we've come through so much! This can't be the end.'

'You never wanted to come in the first place,' moaned Esmeralda. 'I think you were probably right, Trun. You should have stayed home with your cabbages.'

'No, I shouldn't,' Trundle said determinedly. He looked sternly at Percy. 'Let's forget about Sunsett for the moment,' he said. 'What about the first part of the rhyme? The part about a place called Trembling Plain. Percy – do you know where Trembling Plain is at all?'

'No, I don't,' sighed Percy. But a sudden light flickered in his eyes and he sat up straight in his chair. 'But the Dean of Forgotten Geography might!'

'Then let's go and ask him,' said Trundle. He ambled around the desk and popped the Crown of Wood back into its box. 'And let's take this with us, just in case we need to refer to the rhyme again.'

Esmeralda gazed at him, a small smile curling at one corner of her snout. 'Who made you boss all of a sudden, Trundle?' she asked.

'Well, someone needs to buck us all up,' Trundle replied. 'You two are acting like this is a wet Monday night in Port Shiverstones!'

'The lad's right!' said Percy, getting up and tightening the rope belt around his middle. 'While there's life, there's hope, eh, Trundle?'

'Exactly!' said Trundle.

'Follow me!' pronounced the newly revived Herald Persuivant as he marched to the door. 'The Dean will most likely be in the Orrery Chamber. If there is such a place as Trembling Plain in Sundered Lands, he'll know of it for sure!'

'Lawks!' gasped Trundle. 'What's *that*?'

He had good reason to be astounded at the sight that met them as the Herald Persuivant opened the tall door that led to the Orrery Chamber.

It was a huge circular room like a conservatory, made up mostly of windows and with a high domed roof of glass panels through which the sun shone brightly. Beneath the tall windows, cabinets and

22

bookcases and tables and lecterns circled the walls, but dominating the whole of the middle of the room was a massive contraption the like of which Trundle had never seen in his entire life.

'This,' beamed Percy, gesturing up at the vast device as he ushered Trundle and Esmeralda into the chamber, 'is the Great Orrery, the pride of the Worshipful Guild of Observators, and one of the Nine Wonders of the Sundered Lands!'

'Not bad,' said Esmeralda, gazing up at the machine. 'Not bad at all!'

The colossal Orrery was supported on a heavy pillar of black wrought iron from which thick, twisted metal cables stretched down, bolting the entire shuddering thing to the floor. High above their heads, great arms and levers revolved, jutting out like spokes from a hub of cogwheels and gears and ratchets and sprockets that squealed and squeaked and clanged and hummed and whirred and rumbled.

Trundle guessed that there must be over a thousand metal arms projecting out from the top of the machine, all of different lengths and all moving at different speeds. And hanging from each arm was a globe, some made of iron, some of brass or copper or bronze, others of gold and silver and lead.

And endlessly circling the foot of the iron pillar, six weasels on bicycles attached to great clanking chains pedalled away to provide the power that operated the whole towering device.

A number of important-looking badgers in purple robes were busy at desks and lecterns, scribbling intently in large ledgers.

'What is it for?' Trundle breathed as he stared up at the constantly revolving balls of shining metal.

'It's an accurate model of every inhabited and charted island in the whole of the Sundered Lands,' Percy explained. He pointed to a large golden ball moving in a slow, majestic circle close to the centre of the machine. 'That is Widdershins,' he said. He pointed again. 'And over there are Neep and Willowland and Wildrock.' He stabbed his finger to and fro. 'And Drumcloggit and Skine and Hernswick and Drune.' He pointed to a portly old badger with a fur-lined gown of purple silk. 'That is the Orrery Master,' he said. 'Every evening it is his solemn duty to bring the Orrery to a halt and to fetch ladders and to take rulers and callipers and other measuring devices and make scores of tiny but vital adjustments, so that the Orrery is always one hundred per cent accurate.'

Esmeralda stared at him. 'You mean they have

to tinker with this thing every single night?' she asked incredulously. 'That's got to be the most mind-boggling waste of time ever!'

Percy frowned. 'The quest for scientific perfection is never a waste of time, young lady,' he said firmly.

'Says you!' retorted Esmeralda.

'Is the Dean of Forgotten Geography here?' asked Trundle, anxious to prevent an argument between his friends.

'Yes he is, come along with me,' Percy said, a little sharply, Trundle thought. 'And, Esmeralda, please try not to tell the Dean that his life's work is entirely meaningless, if you can manage that.'

'I'll do my best,' she replied genially. 'But it won't be easy!'

They came upon the Dean of Forgotten Geography, rummaging through the lower shelves of a bookcase and mumbling to himself.

He was an elderly and rather frail-looking badger with a grey muzzle and huge pale watery eyes that peered weakly from behind thick spectacles.

'My most convivial greetings to you, my dear Dean,' said Percy, speaking in a very formal and rather pompous voice.

'And to you, Herald,' replied the Dean, straightening up with a creak and a grimace. 'And what brings you to this far-flung corner of the guild, my dear sir?'

'Something of great interest and moment has come to my attention, Dean,' Percy pronounced, taking the wooden box from Trundle's hands. 'Something which I feel certain will pique your academic interest.'

'Indeed, my good Herald?' asked the Dean. 'And, pray, what might that be?'

'This receptacle contains a piece of parchment

upon which has been inscribed an alliterative fragment of doggerel which I firmly believe—'

'Oh, will you pair of old fogies cut the cackle, please!' interrupted Esmeralda, snatching the box from Percy's hands and tipping the lid up. 'Just read the poem, Dean,' she said. 'And then tell us— *uh-oh*!'

Trundle stared uneasily at her. 'Uh-oh?' he said. 'What kind of uh-oh?'

A moment later he knew exactly what kind of *uh-oh* it was as the wooden box began to shudder and strain in Esmeralda's arms. There was a fizzing sound and a hissing sound and suddenly a ball of blue fire leaped out of the box, spinning up into the air and shooting out bolts of vivid blue lightning in all directions. The Crown of Wood had come alive again!

'Goodness gracious!' pronounced the Dean, his spectacles falling from his snout. 'May I enquire the purpose of this unparalleled exhibition, my dear Herald?'

'Later, Dean. For the moment, I suggest we all take cover!' yelled Percy, grabbing the Dean and diving under a nearby desk. Bolts of sizzling lightning were careering backwards and forwards and upwards and downwards through the huge chamber, spitting and roaring and shedding sparks as they collided and ricocheted at dizzying speed.

Trundle winced as he saw several streaks of blue lightning strike the machinery at the top of the Orrery. The effect was startling. The whole cumbersome device began to speed up, the helpless cycling weasels yelling and shrieking as their little legs went pumping up and down faster and faster on the pedals of their out-of-control bicycles.

And as Trundle watched, the hanging globes began to spin in an ever widening arc, blue lightning flickering from ball to ball while more lightning crackled along the arms and in among the intricate mechanism.

The Orrery spun faster and faster. The metal balls became entangled with one another and a few broke loose and went crashing through the windows like cannonballs. Smoke rose from the hub of the device. Cogwheels and sprockets showered down like shrapnel. The whine of the spinning machine turned to a demented howl.

And then, with a final shriek of over-burdened gears and shearing pinwheels, the whirling Orrery started to fly apart.

'Everybody down!' yelled Esmeralda.

Trundle didn't need telling twice.

As he lay there on his face, with his arms up over his head and with total mayhem breaking out above him, it struck him that 'uh-oh' had probably been a bit of an understatement.

Forgotten Geography

The horrible grinding and screeching of the exploding machinery filled Trundle's ears as he lay on the floor of the wrecked Orrery Chamber. Globes and levers and cogs and gears bounced all around him, and playing over everything was the sizzling and spitting blue lightning that had caused all the chaos.

He lifted his head, worried for Esmeralda. She

was sitting under a lectern with her hands over her ears and her eyes screwed shut. Something came bouncing across the floor towards her, spraying blue sparks.

'Watch out!' Trundle cried.

Esmeralda's eyes snapped open and she gave a yelp of alarm, holding out her arms to fend off the object.

She seemed as surprised as Trundle, as the glowing ball plopped neatly into her two paws, smoking a little and making a soft whirring noise.

'Oh, well held!' gasped Trundle, lifting himself up as Esmeralda sat blinking at the dented brass ball resting quietly between her hands.

The Orrery Chamber was a terrible mess. Several of the windows had been shattered, and there was debris all over the floor from the ruined remnants of the Orrery. The great device itself stood at a crazy angle, its arms bent and buckled, its few remaining globes all tangled up together. Among the rubble, the six weasel cyclists could be seen staggering around in circles and falling over. Here and there, purple-robed badgers were picking themselves up with dazed expressions.

Percy crawled out from under the desk and slammed the lid down on the wooden box.

The Orrery Master was standing ankle deep in bits of machinery, staring up with anguished eyes at the steaming remnants of his beloved device, whimpering a little and gnawing distractedly at a leather-bound ledger which he was twisting between his hands.

'Great merciful Fates!' gasped a voice as the Dean of Forgotten Geography emerged from under the desk on hands and knees. 'My good Herald! What in all of Sundered Lands have you done!'

'It was an accident, I can assure you, my very good Dean,' said Percy as he helped the elderly

gentleman to his feet. 'Most regrettable. Entirely
unforeseeable! I had no idea . . . really – no slightest
expectation!'

'That *was* pretty spectacular!' gasped
Esmeralda, scrambling up. She stared at the brass ball
between her paws. ' And I don't think it was no
accident, Perce!' she added, grinning wildly. 'It was the
Fates what did this, and no mistake!' She brandished
the globe under his snout. 'All this was meant to
happen – which means I was meant to be given *this*.'
She turned to the bewildered Dean. 'Tell me quickly
now, which island does this represent?'

The Dean blinked at her. 'I beg your pardon?'
he gasped, as though he could hardly believe his ears.

'Listen, Grandpa,' Esmeralda said, rather rudely
Trundle thought. 'I'm betting every prickle on my head
that the Crown of Stone is on the island represented by
this ball of brass. So – come on – which one is it?'

'She could very well be right, Dean,' added Percy, taking the ball from Esmeralda and handing it to the shaky-pawed old Dean. 'Which island is it?'

As though in a dream, the Dean took the battered ball and turned it slowly in his paws, peering intently at it. 'There should be a serial number,' he muttered. 'Around the equator. But I'd need my spectacles . . .'

'Oh, give it back here,' said Esmeralda, snatching the ball. 'Yes! Here we are! The number is six three nine four five two seven seven eight zero four two six eight one four three two seven six nine zero two two two five three seven eight.'

'It's intact,' said the Dean, 'that's good – but to find the identity of the island in question, we will need to consult the comprehensive compendia in the Antechamber of Geographic Certitudes.' He gazed around himself. 'But really . . . it seems somewhat incongruous to be doing such research while the poor Orrery Master has suffered such a catastrophic disaster!'

'There is little to be done for the Orrery Master at the moment,' said Percy, ushering the Dean towards a small side-door. 'And the finding of the island may lead to one of the most important scientific discoveries of the past two thousand years, my good Dean!'

'Oh? Indeed?' said the Dean. 'Well, in that case . . . '

The Dean opened the door and led them into a small antechamber. Esmeralda and Trundle whipped through and Percy closed the door firmly on their backs, shutting out the pitiful sobbing of the Orrery Master.

The Dean gave Percy a concerned look. 'Should you not first of all explain to me what just happened, my dear Herald? The object in that box is clearly a source of great potency. From whence does it come and what is its purpose?'

'I shall write a treatise on it, my good Dean,' Percy said briskly. 'And you shall be the first to read it, I can assure you. In the meantime, what of the island?'

'Well, now,' said the Dean, turning and walking along a bookcase filled with huge old tomes. 'The prefix six three nine four means that we need to look in Pountney's *Guide to Dull Places*.'

The Dean fetched some stepladders on wheels. He climbed to a high shelf and perused the books up there while Esmeralda read out the numbers again.

'I have it!' the Dean said at last, heaving a book off the shelf and tottering down the steps with it in his arms.

He took the book to a lectern and, slipping white kid gloves on to his hands, he opened it and carefully turned the pages. He had Esmeralda recite

the numbers yet again as he turned
page after page.

'Here it is!'
the Dean said,
leaning close
and adjusting

his spectacles. 'Oh dear me, what a disappointment.'

'Don't tell me it doesn't exist any more!'
groaned Esmeralda.

'Oh, it exists, sure enough,' said the Dean. 'But
it's a miserable flat little island. There's nothing of
interest there at all. It's well off the main trading routes
– very dull indeed. It's called Trembling Plain.'

'That's the place mentioned in the rhyme!'
Trundle yelled excitedly. 'Esmeralda, you were right!
The Fates are still on our side!'

'So, where is this island, Mr Dean, mate?' asked
Esmeralda. 'And how do we get there?'

The Dean peered at her. 'I have no idea, young lady,' he said. 'You would need to consult the Orrery to learn that.'

'What?' howled Trundle and Esmeralda in chorus.

'Oh, no!' groaned Percy, his hand to his brow.

'I'm sure the Master will put the Orrery back together again as quickly as he can,' said the Dean.

'And how quickly might that be?' asked Trundle.

'I would imagine it will be up and running again within a hundred years,' said the Dean. 'It's a tricky business, you know. He will need to consult all the old archives.'

'We don't have *a hundred years*, matey!' howled Esmeralda. 'We're on a deadline here – and there are pirates and evil aunts to worry about.'

'Is there no other way of learning more of this

island, my dear Dean?' asked Percy.

The Dean frowned. 'Well, this book *is* over a thousand years old,' he said. 'It's quite possible that the island has a different name these days. Many do, you know – the history of etymology is a most fascinating subject. For instance—'

'Never mind all that!' shrieked Esmeralda. 'How do we find out what the island is called *now*?'

'By consulting Doctor Gleek's *Relegated Atlas*,' said the Dean.

They waited impatiently while he fetched the book in question.

Trundle could see that even Percy was boiling over with the suspense as the old Dean worked his way slowly through the atlas.

'Here's the entry,' said the Dean at long last. 'Well, well, I was right! Trembling Plain became Quivering Plain about nine hundred years ago. And

41

then, two centuries later, it says here that the island was being called Quiverplain.'

'Not helping!' growled Esmeralda.

'And then, about five hundred years ago, the authorities altered the name to Quiverstones,' the Dean continued. 'And finally, not much over a hundred years ago, the name was finally changed to Shiverstones.'

'Shiverstones?' hooted Trundle. 'You mean the sixth crown is in *Shiverstones*???'

'Bless my soul!' gasped Percy.

'Right back where we started!' squealed Esmeralda. 'Wheee-oooh! Who'd have thought it?'

The distant, dull, sonorous clanging of a bell broke into their astonishment.

'Ahh, the Cloister Tocsin,' said the Dean. 'Word must have spread of the disaster with the Orrery. No doubt Professor Brockwise will wish to see us all and learn how the catastrophe came about.'

He adjusted his spectacles. 'The Highmost Chancellor will be most interested in the contents of that box, to be sure!'

'Lawks!' exclaimed Esmeralda. 'That'll never do! We have to get out of here!'

'No, no, child,' said Percy. 'We shall take the box straight to His Nibs. As the Dean says, Professor Brockwise will be most fascinated to learn what we have within!'

Trundle felt he should point out that this was probably a really bad idea. Last time they met up with the Highmost Chancellor, he chased them with his stick and set the guards on them. But before he could speak, Percy turned his back on the Dean and gave them a long slow wink.

'Oh, yes!' said Esmeralda, catching on straight away. 'Let's do exactly that.'

'I think we'll take the back way,' Percy said,

heading for a door in the far wall of the small antechamber. 'It'll be quicker.'

And before the Dean was given the chance to say anything more, the three of them had whisked out through the door and were pattering at quite a speed along a deserted corridor.

'Where are we *really* going?' asked Trundle.

'My private quarters,' puffed Percy. 'If we're going to get away from here and find that last crown, we'll need to be sharp! His Nibs may be a doddery old twit, but even he has the wits to have us arrested while he finds out what happened to the Orrery.'

'Uh, Perce?' asked Esmeralda. 'When you say "we" – do you mean you're coming with us?'

Percy smiled at her. 'If you'll have me,' he said.

'You bet we will!' said Trundle. That was the best news he'd heard for a long time. With a total brainbox like Percy on board, nothing could stop them.

The final crown was all but theirs!

And to think – after all their racing about across the length and width of the Sundered Lands, that the Crown of Stone should have been in Shiverstones all along!

Amazing!

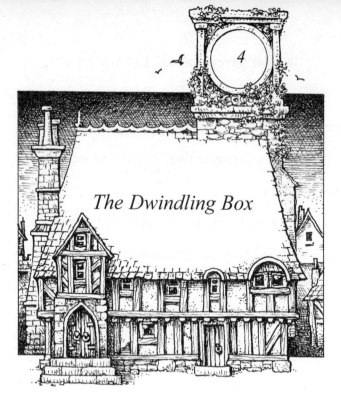

The Dwindling Box

Trundle was surprised by the gloominess of Percy's private quarters. The main room that he showed them into was fusty and dusty and musty and cobwebby. The windows were grimy and the shabby furniture was of sombre colours.

'You actually live here, Percy?' asked Esmeralda, staring around with a wrinkling snout.

'Indeed,' Percy replied. 'I'm lucky. College Fellows of lesser importance have much more depressing quarters.'

'Hard to imagine that,' Esmeralda muttered under her breath.

For Trundle the most disturbing thing in the room was the heavy carved frieze that ran around the top of the walls. It was made of black wood and depicted a host of strange and unsettling creatures. The statuettes that Trundle liked least of all were the ravens – there were a lot of them – grim-looking birds, many chipped or broken or with missing heads and wings, staring down at them with their beady black eyes and looking a little too realistic for his liking!

'If we're doing a flit, we ought to take the crowns with us, Percy,' said Esmeralda.

'So we shall,' agreed the Herald, opening a cupboard and rummaging about in it, flinging out odds and ends as he waded deeper in.

'How are we going to carry them about?'
Trundle asked. 'I mean – without them doing that *thing*
they do when they're together?' He looked at
Esmeralda. 'Could you use some of your Roamany
magic to keep them quiet?' he asked.

'That's a bit out of my league, Trun,' said
Esmeralda, rubbing her snout.

Percy emerged from the cupboard, festooned in
cobwebs and with a carpetbag in his hands.
Embroidered on the bag were the large letters GP.

'What's GP stand for, Percy?' asked Trundle.

'Oh!' Percy said, seeming a little flustered. 'It
stands for . . . *Gerald Persuivant*. A long time ago,
there was a Herald called Gerald – this was his bag.'

'It's not going to be big enough for all the
crowns,' commented Esmeralda.

'That's not what it's for at all,' said Percy,

placing the carpetbag on the floor and opening it. He pulled out a crossbow and a quiver of small arrows. Trundle and Esmeralda gazed at the weapon in surprise.

'Expecting trouble, are you, Percy?' asked Esmeralda.

'You never know when you might run into something nasty,' said Percy, replacing the crossbow and the quiver in the bag. 'After all, there are pirates on our trail, aren't there?'

Trundle had to admit he had a point, but that didn't make it any less odd that a chap like Percy should have a crossbow in his cupboard in the first place!

'And I think I can come up with a way of safely transporting the crowns,' Percy said cheerfully. He vanished into the cupboard again and reappeared carrying a square box.

He placed the box on a small round table.

'Gather around, my little friends,' he said. 'This unusual item is known as the Dwindling Box.'

The box was made of brass and ivory, carved all over with curious symbols and designs, worn smooth by the passage of time.

'The Dwindling Box has been in my possession for a long, long time,' Percy told them. 'It has come in very useful in the past.'

'What does it do?' asked Trundle.

'I will show you,' said Percy. He unlatched the lid and tipped it open. 'Hand me the Crown of Wood, Esmeralda,' he said.

Looking puzzled, Esmeralda gave the box with the crown in it to the Herald. It seemed to Trundle that the Dwindling Box was probably just about big enough to hold the Crown of Wood. But what about the other four? Where was Percy planning on putting them?

Percy took the Crown of Wood out of its box and dropped it into the Dwindling Box.

'OK,' said Esmeralda dubiously. 'So far so good. Where do the rest go?'

Chuckling to himself, Percy gestured for them to draw close and look into the Dwindling Box.

'Oh my!' gasped Trundle, staring in amazement at the tiny wooden crown that sat in the bottom of the box. It was no bigger than an eggcup!

'Oh, wow, Percy!' Esmeralda breathed. 'It's magic!'

'Of a kind,' said Percy. 'As soon as we're ready to leave, we'll make our way back to my office to pick up the other crowns. I'm pretty certain that once they're inside the Dwindling Box, their powers will be easily contained. But we'll need to keep the lid well-fastened, just to be on the safe side!'

'Well done, Percy,' said Esmeralda admiringly.

'And I thought only the Roamany people had magic!'

'If this *is* magic, then it's an older and deeper magic than your hedgerow tricks!' said Percy as he snapped the lid of the box shut.

Trundle saw Esmeralda shoot their friend an annoyed look – but Percy was smiling affably at her and she didn't say anything.

'Well now,' said Percy. 'I think it's about time we got out of here, don't you? As soon as he realizes I'm missing, His Nibs will have guards racing about all over, searching every nook and cranny for me!'

'*The Thief in the Night* isn't too far away,' said Esmeralda. 'Once we have the rest of the crowns, we could be there in a few minutes.'

'Excellent!' beamed Percy. 'Trundle, my boy, I'm putting you in charge of the Dwindling Box. Keep it safe!'

'Shiverstones, here we come!' declared Esmeralda. 'And quest's end!'

Trundle picked up the Dwindling Box, thrilled to think they had nearly fulfilled their mission, and wondering what would happen when the six crowns were finally brought together.

They headed out of the room, but just as Trundle was closing the door behind them, he heard an odd flapping sound. Puzzled, he popped his head around the door just in time to see one of the ravens from the wall-frieze go flapping out through an open window!

'Hey, you!' he shouted. 'Come back here!'

'What is it?' asked Percy, turning back.

'One of those raven statues wasn't a statue at all!' yelled Trundle, running to the window. 'It was real.'

'It was spying on us!' cried Esmeralda. 'It was a

filthy rotten spy!' She looked at Percy, who had joined them at the window. 'The pirates use ravens as messengers! And that bird overheard everything we were talking about!'

They watched as the big black bird went flapping away over the spires and towers of the college. As it shrank into the distance, Trundle heard a faint croaking voice calling back to him, 'You'll get yours, matey! You see if you don't!'

'We have even less time than I thought,' said Percy. 'We need to fetch the other four crowns and get out of here as quick as lightning!' He shuddered. 'I don't like the idea of us having *The Iron Pig* on our trail,' he said. 'I don't like it one little bit!'

Percy led them along many an empty corridor and up and down several deserted flights of back-stairs in order to get them to his office without them being spotted. Once or twice, they had to backtrack or dive into cover when a posse of guards came pounding down a corridor or could be heard clanking along around a corner.

But at last they found themselves in his office, stepping carefully through the debris left from their previous visit.

Trundle placed the Dwindling Box on the desk; he clicked the latch and opened the lid. Percy took the Crown of Ice out of its container and popped it inside the box. Trundle peered in, smiling to see the tiny Crown of Ice sitting quietly beside the tiny Crown of Wood.

Esmeralda fetched the Crown of Fire out of the cupboard while Percy rescued the Crown of Iron from the wall cabinet.

Soon, the two other crowns were nestling in the bottom of the box. Now it only remained for Percy to take down the Crown of Crystal from its high shelf and drop it into the Dwindling Box.

Trundle cringed a little as the fifth crown joined the others – half expecting some kind of alarming reaction to follow. But nothing did. Percy had been right – whatever made the Dwindling Box work, it was also keeping the crowns under control. With a relieved sigh, Trundle shut the box and clicked the latch.

Now all they had to do was to get to *The Thief in the Night* without walking into any trouble.

Picking up the carpetbag, Percy headed for the door with Esmeralda and Trundle close on his heels.

He opened the door just as a large fox guard was about to grab the handle on the outside.

'Here!' exclaimed the surprised guard. 'I've got orders to take you to the Highmost Chancellor, Mister Herald Persuivant, sir.'

'Have you indeed, my good fellow?' replied

Percy as though nothing out of the ordinary was going

on. 'I shall be most delighted to comply with Doctor

Brockwise's wishes.' He glanced down. 'Your bootlace

is undone, Sergeant Fawkes. Doctor Brockwise doesn't

approve of sloppily dressed guards, you know!'

The guard stared down at his feet. 'Wotcher talkin' about?' he said in a puzzled voice. 'My bootlace ain't undone at all.'

'My mistake!' said Percy, swinging the carpetbag on high. To Trundle's total astonishment, he brought it down with a hefty whack on the guard's bowed head.

Sergeant Fawkes hit the floor like a sack of cabbages.

'Help me get him inside,' puffed Percy.

'Crikey, Perce!' gasped Esmeralda. 'Look what you did!'

'Desperate times call for desperate measures,' said Percy, peering cautiously up and down the corridor as the three of them grabbed the guard and dragged him into the room.

Trundle had to agree that Percy was right about

that – all the same, it was rather startling the way he had knocked poor old Fawkes out. It seemed that there was more to their friend the Herald Persuivant than met the eye!

Evening was falling and *The Thief in the Night* was racing across the darkening sky with its sails full of a good, strong wind.

Away behind them, Widdershins could still be seen as a grey blob. Ahead of them, the sun was slowly setting behind the dark mass of Nightreef, sending out a final few shafts of golden light as it disappeared.

Nightreef! Once a day the huge solid barrier of broken rocks and rubble would circle the sun, blocking out the daylight and giving the people of Sundered Lands their dark and starry nights.

Just a few hours ago, and without any more awkward encounters, the gallant little skyboat had gone skimming away from the grounds of the college. But Trundle still felt uneasy; he sat in the stern, clinging on to the tiller and peering over his shoulder all the time, fearful that at any moment the blood-red sails of *The Iron Pig* would hove into view behind them.

And then he really did see something! A small dark shape away in the distance. He puckered his brows, watching the thing as it got closer, changing from a dot to a blob to a recognizable winged shape.

'It's the raven!' he yelled, pointing back. 'It's coming for us!'

Percy and Esmeralda looked up.

'I don't think so,' Percy said, peering back along their course. 'No, you're quite wrong, my boy. That's no raven. That's just a good honest blackbird going about its business.' He patted Trundle on the head. 'I think you're getting a little bit jumpy, my lad.'

'He does do that,' agreed Esmeralda.

Trundle frowned as the black shape curved away through the evening air and was lost behind a cloudbank.

It had looked *very* like a raven, whatever Percy said. But Trundle decided it wasn't worth arguing about it.

But he still had a nasty prickly sensation in the back of his neck, and the horrible feeling that danger wasn't far away. After all, where there were ravens, could Captain Grizzletusk and the ghastly *Iron Pig* be far behind?

5

Furrowman's Hat

Despite all of Trundle's fears, the little skyboat made it to Shiverstones without further incident.

It was a bright, clear morning as they came circling down over Port Shiverstones. Beyond the huddled town, acres and acres of stubby cabbages stretched out over the flat, windswept island like a huge green carpet.

Trundle gazed down at his homeland with very mixed feelings. For a long time, his only thought had been to get back home and to bolt his front door against the world and to sit at peace beside a roaring fire.

But now, the inner Trundle – the adventurous part of him – was wide-awake and restless, and as they glided in for the landing it was whispering in his ear: *Cabbages and cabbages and cabbages! There's more to life than trimming the wicks of Port Shiverstones' lamps, you know! Out out, bold Trundle, or your life will be but a walking shadow!*

'Hmm, very poetic,' Trundle mumbled.

'What was that, Trun?' asked Esmeralda as she turned the tiller and brought the trim craft around to lean into the wind.

'Nothing,' Trundle said briskly, resting a paw on top of the Dwindling Box. 'Nothing at all.' He pushed his gloomy thoughts away – they were almost at quest's end! By the end of the day, they might have all six crowns in their hands! *Think about that!*

The area around the docks still showed signs of the damage inflicted on the town by the attack of Grizzletusk's pirates. Some of the jetties were broken or badly scorched, and a few warehouses and other buildings were no more than burned-out hulks. But Trundle could see that the normal life of the port was carrying on despite the disruption. Several merchant windships were moored alongside the remaining jetties, and there was plenty of activity as cargoes were loaded and unloaded, sending cabbages to all the far-flung islands of the Sundered Lands, and bringing in all the goods and equipment and paraphernalia that made life bearable in Shiverstones.

Esmeralda steered the skyboat to a soft landing at the far end of a busy jetty. Percy stepped off and looped the mooring rope around a bollard. A few moments later, the three of them were walking down the jetty, attracting a few curious glances from the dockworkers and windship crews who heaved on ropes and hauled on cables to load and unload the gently bobbing vessels.

'Well now, my boy,' said Percy as they walked on through the docks. 'Where would you suggest we begin the search?'

Trundle blinked at him. 'I don't have the faintest idea,' he admitted.

'Come on, Trun,' added Esmeralda. 'You've lived here all your life. Rattle a few brain cells, there's a good fellow.'

Trundle frowned, trying to imagine where the simple, down-to-earth folk of Port Shiverstones might keep such a curious but impractical item as a stone crown. Knowing them, it could be lying forgotten in a

ditch, or it could have been broken up to mend a wall –
or it might just as easily be sitting unnoticed on
someone's mantelpiece or tucked away in the back of a
cupboard!

'Morning, young Boldoak,' called a heavy-set
beaver in a frockcoat and top hat as he waddled self-
importantly towards them. 'We thought the pirates had
got you, for sure!'

'No, they didn't get me, Alderman Firkinpole,'
Trundle called back. 'I've been on a quest, you know!
A very important quest.'

'Have you indeed?' The Alderman paused and
gave the three a curious look. 'Well, now you're back,
I hope you'll be lighting the lamps again. It was so
dark down Savoy Street last night, I tripped over the
kerb and bruised my nose! Your father would never
have abandoned his duties to go a-gallivanting.'

'Sorry about that, Alderman,' stammered Trundle.

'Sorry boils no cabbage leaves, young man,' scolded the Alderman. 'You just attend to your duties.' And with that, the portly beaver stumped away.

'Why didn't you tell him to take a running jump, Trun?' asked Esmeralda.

Trundle gave her an appalled look. 'That was Alderman Firkinpole,' he explained. 'I can't tell Alderman Firkinpole to take a running jump.'

Esmeralda shook her head very slowly. 'When are you going to get it into your head that you're a big international hero, Trundle? You've been to places these country bumpkins have never even dreamed of! You've found five of the six lost crowns! You're not silly old Trundle any more. You're Boldoak the Brave!'

'Yes, you're right,' said Trundle. 'I know you're right.'

'So, the next time someone tries to tell you off, give them a piece of your mind.'

'I will!' Trundle declared. 'You'll see!'

'Hoi, Trundle, you podgy twerp!' shouted a woman's voice from a nearby shop front. 'We haven't had a light in the streets for weeks! When are you going to get back to work, you lazy idle loafer?'

'As soon as possible, Miss Buckfur,' Trundle called back.

'I should hope so!' declared the shopkeeper. 'It's a disgrace!' And with that, she slammed into her shop so that the glass rattled in the windows.

Trundle noticed Percy smiling behind his paw, and he could see Esmeralda rolling her eyes.

'She was an old friend of my mother's,' he explained. 'I was only being polite.' His face rosy with embarrassment, he marched off across the open dock-front and headed into the town.

His friends didn't seem to realize how hard it was for him to still be Trundle the Hero now that he

OPENING
HOURS

was back among people who had only known him as amiable and harmless young Trundle the Lamplighter.

But an idea had come to him.

'We should go and speak with all the old folk,' he suggested. 'We have families here that came to Shiverstones with Furrowman Plowplodder, hundreds of years ago. You never know, some of them might remember old stories that mention stone crowns.'

'That sounds like a very sensible option,' said Percy. 'Lead on, my lad – lead on!'

It was a forlorn and discouraged trio of adventurers who sat on the steps under the statue of Furrowman Plowplodder in Market Square at the end of a long and fruitless day.

They had traipsed all over Port Shiverstones, speaking to anyone who would listen, asking about the Crown of Stone till they were weary and footsore.

Most people they approached had never heard of the Crown, and those few who had, told them that the Crowns of the Badger Lords of Old only existed in nursery tales.

There never were any Badger Lords! they were confidently told. *Magic crowns, indeed! What a silly idea!* the good folk of Port Shiverstones often added. *When will you stop all this nonsense and get back to lighting the lamps at night, Trundle?* they frequently finished.

'No one knows nuffin'!' mumbled Esmeralda, her chin in her paws. 'We've wasted the whole day!'

'But the rhyme means the crown must surely be here,' said Percy. 'It's just a case of finding it.'

'Harrumph!' said Esmeralda and Trundle in chorus.

There were very few people about by now, and everyone was hurrying homewards as the light failed.

Trundle cast a bleak eye over the unlit lamps and gave a long sigh.

'Young Boldoak?' enquired a sharp voice. 'What are you doing here? I thought you were dead!'

Trundle and the others looked up. Trundle recognized the rather dapper rabbit who had spoken to him. It was Hedgeley Twiddle, the Clerk of Works from Shiverstones Town Hall, and he looked somewhat cross.

'No, Mr Clerk of Works, sir,' said Trundle. 'I'm not dead.'

'Well, that's very inconvenient,' declared the Clerk. 'I've had you officially certified as dead, with the assumption that you were murdered by pirates. Do you realize how much paperwork you are going to cause me?'

'I'm sure he's really sorry to put you out by being alive,' Esmeralda said caustically. 'The pirates are still after him, if that's any comfort. Maybe he'll still get killed and save you all that work.'

The Clerk gave her a kindly look. 'Well, that's a possibility, I suppose,' he said affably. 'Not that I'd wish you dead, Trundle.'

'Thanks,' Trundle said heavily. 'Much obliged, I'm sure.'

'I imagine you have your hands full, my good sir,' said Percy. 'What with all the mess and mayhem caused by the pirates.'

'Oh, there's plenty to be done, for sure,' said the Clerk. 'But you know, in some ways, it was a blessing in disguise.'

'It must have been a very *good* disguise,' Trundle said in astonishment. 'What can you possibly mean?'

'It gave us the chance to do some renovating,' replied the Clerk. 'Especially in the area of the docks.

And the town did need a good spring-clean.' He
pointed up at the statue of the founder of Shiverstones.
'Why, we're even planning on giving old Furrowman
here a good sprucing-up. Tsk! Look at all the soot and
grime on that spiky hat of his!'

'Hmm,' said Trundle.

'Well, I can't stand here gossiping,' announced
the Clerk of Works. 'There's a Cabbagegrower Caucus
to chair, and I can't be late.' So saying, he turned on
his heel and toddled off into the gathering darkness.

'Ummm . . . Percy? Trundle?' murmured
Esmeralda, staring up at the old stone statue of
Furrowman Plowplodder.

'What?' Trundle sighed.

'Would the two of you care to take a look at the
spiky hat that fellow was just talking about?'

Trundle and Percy looked up at the statue on its
square plinth.

'Bless my soul!' gasped Percy. 'I can't believe it!'

'Lawks!' choked Trundle, scrambling to his feet, his eyes goggling in disbelief.

A wide, slow smile spread over Esmeralda's face. 'Spiky hat, my prickles!' she laughed. 'That there hat is for sure and definite a *crown*!'

She was right. Trundle could see it straight away now it had been pointed out to him.

Furrowman Plowplodder's spiky hat was undoubtedly the Crown of Stone.

6

Cut-throats and Villains!

'I simply can't believe you sometimes, Trundle!' Esmeralda said in exasperation. 'You've lived here all your life! Have you never looked at that statue? Did you *never* realize that Furrowman Plowplodder was wearing a crown?'

'Well, no,' replied Trundle. 'I didn't. I don't think anyone ever really looked properly at it.

It was just . . . sort of . . . *there*.'

Percy was sitting under the statue, slapping his knees and laughing heartily.

'My, my,' he said, wiping a tear away. 'What an extraordinary end to the quest! To think the Crown of Stone has been right here under Trundle's nose all the time! Extraordinary! Most amusing!' He started laughing again, and pretty soon Esmeralda and Trundle were laughing along with him.

It was as the Herald Persuivant said, the most ludicrous and hilarious end to the quest that Trundle could possibly have imagined.

'Someone had better climb up and fetch it, hadn't they, Trundle?' said Esmeralda once they had all finished laughing.

'Yes,' Trundle said. 'And I suppose by *someone* you mean *me*! Well, don't worry, this time I'll be happy to oblige.'

It wasn't an especially tall statue, and it didn't take Trundle long to clamber up and lift the Crown of Stone from around Furrowman Plowplodder's brow. Luckily it came away fairly easily . . .

The only slight problem came when he returned to the ground. The Shiverstones evening had darkened to a starry night and not a single lamp in the Market Square was lit to shed any light by which they could examine the crown.

'I think there might be some words inscribed around the inside,' said Percy, peering with narrowed eyes.

'Hold on and I'll conjure up a palm-light for us,' said Esmeralda.

'Oh, I don't think you'll be needing that, my dears,' said a genial and horribly familiar voice. A moment later, Esmeralda's Aunt Millie Rose Thorne stepped out from behind the statue with a big, sneering raven perched on her shoulder. 'I'll be taking that crown, dearies,' Aunt Millie continued. 'If you don't object at all, that is!'

The three of them sprang back in shock and alarm, Trundle's paw reaching for the hilt of his sword.

'I told you you'd get yours!' croaked the raven, giving Trundle a very dirty look. Trundle was quite certain that this was the same raven that had overheard them in the Herald Persuivant's office. So, it wasn't in the employ of the pirates at all, it was working for Esmeralda's treacherous aunt!

'Millie Rose Thorne, you will not get your hands on this crown,' shouted Percy, clutching the Crown of Stone tightly to his chest. 'Nor on any of the others!'

'Oh, but I think you'll find I will!' Aunt Millie retorted, her eyes glittering greedily.

'Never!' shouted Trundle, whipping his sword

out and leaping between the wicked Roamany Queen and his companions. 'Get back, you wretched excuse for an aunt!' he yelled, waving the sword in front of her. 'So, you think you can just take it off us, do you? You and whose army?'

'Her and *my* army,' growled a new voice from out of the darkness.

'Oh, blimey!' exclaimed Esmeralda as Captain Grizzletusk stepped forward from deep shadows. 'That's all we needed!'

The dreaded pirate captain wasn't alone.

Not by a long way, he wasn't. Trundle and Esmeralda and Percy shrank together as dozens and dozens of fearsome pirates appeared out of the gloom, armed with muskets and pistols and blunderbusses. The three adventurers were surrounded!

'Wotcher, shipmates!' cackled an evil voice. 'Come on in – yer time's up!' It was Captain Slaughter, the one-eyed and peg-legged raven, perched as always on the shoulder of Razorback, the bloodthirsty bo'sun of *The Iron Pig*.

'I'm surprised you lot are prepared to show your ugly mugs around us, considering the beating you got the last time we met,' remarked Esmeralda, sounding as cool as a cucumber.

'It'll be different this time, my lovelies,' growled Razorback, his eyes glinting with malice. 'This time we're going to chop you into so many portions that even your own mothers wouldn't be able to put you back together again.'

Millie Rose Thorne smiled wickedly as she moved to stand alongside Captain Grizzletusk. 'We can do this the easy way, or we can do it the hard way,' she said. 'Personally, I quite like the idea of the hard way – but it's up to the three of you.'

'Hand over the crowns and we might let you

live,' snarled Grizzletusk. 'Or, to be more honest with ye, we might let you die quick!'

Oddly enough, the thought that he might come to a grim and grisly end didn't frighten Trundle – it only made him angry and strangely determined. Perhaps he had finally accepted that the Fates were on their side. Or perhaps it was just that if he was going to be killed by pirates, he might as well go down fighting. Besides, a rather brilliant idea had occurred to him.

'You pox-ridden pirates,' he shouted, slicing the air with his sword. 'I'll give you to the count of three to surrender your weapons to us. If you don't, you'll regret it! Those of you who survive, that is!'

There was much chuckling and cackling from the pirates at this. A crooked, fang-toothed smile stretched across Grizzletusk's face. 'I like you,' he snorted, his red eyes burning. 'I think I might keep you as a pet . . . in a little iron cage!'

'Don't say you weren't warned!' began Trundle. 'Three!'

'Steady, Trundle, my boy,' murmured Percy.

'Two!'

'Go get 'em, boys!' snarled Grizzletusk.

'One!' Trundle yelled. And so saying he dropped his sword, picked up the Dwindling Box and unlatched it, tipping it upside down so that the lid fell open. Then he gave the box a good thwack on the bottom.

Five little crowns came tumbling out.

'It's the other crowns!' screeched Esmeralda's aunt. 'Grab them before—'

No one ever found out what she was planning to say next, because as the crowns fell from the box, they began to swell and grow and expand. And as they hit the cobbles, they were back to their proper size and giving off sparks of blue lightning like the centrepiece of a fireworks display.

At the same moment, the Crown of Stone leaped from Percy's hands to join with the others. As hair-raising and alarming as the release of magic had been when *five* crowns were together, it was nothing to the utter chaos that erupted now! Bolts of blue lightning exploded in all directions, whizzing and banging and crackling and hissing as they careered back and forth across the Market Square.

'Fire, you swabs!' howled Captain Grizzletusk. 'Snappily now!'

In response to their captain's orders, nearly every one of the pirates pulled the trigger on their guns.

But they were so blinded by the flashing and flaring and blazing and bursting of the blue lightning, that their shots went wild, missing Trundle and his friends and causing their own shipmates to have to duck and jump aside as the whole of the square was suddenly engulfed in billowing clouds of white gun smoke.

Trundle grabbed up his sword and stumbled around, trying to find Esmeralda and Percy in the dense, swirling smoke.

There was much shouting and wailing from the pirates.

'Argh! I've shot me own toe off!'

'Ouch! It hit me in the eye!'

'Give it back!'

'I can't see a thing!'

'Oi! Watch where you're poking that musket!'

'Careful, you bilge-rat! That's me you're treading on!'

And above all the other voices, Trundle could hear Grizzletusk roaring, 'Don't let 'em get away, you fools! Grab 'em! Nab 'em! Shoot 'em dead and stab 'em!'

'Esmeralda?' Trundle called, stumbling forward with his hands reaching out into the thick smoke. 'Percy? Where are you?'

He bumped into something solid; something that spoke to him. 'Is that you, Trundle, my boy?'

'Yes, Percy!' gasped Trundle. 'Where's Esmeralda?'

'Right here!' A moment later a lemon-coloured palm-light appeared in the smoke and Esmeralda stepped forward. 'That was a great idea, Trun,' she said, beaming from ear to ear. 'But it won't be long before Aunt Millie comes up with a spell to get rid of all this smoke. We need to be gone by then!'

'We must gather up the crowns and put them back in the box,' said Percy. 'Quickly now, before the pirates have time to regroup!'

Esmeralda led them to the bright heart of all the magic. The six crowns had come together in a ring, buzzing and vibrating as shafts and beams and streaks of crackling lightning shot out in every direction.

Percy held back while Esmeralda and Trundle crawled cautiously forward, Trundle holding out the Dwindling Box with its lid open.

One by one, Esmeralda managed to grab the crowns and pop them back into the box. The lightning fizzed and guttered and died away.

'This way,' hissed Percy, snatching up his carpetbag and running ahead of them into the fug.

'Hoi! Mind who you're barging into!' growled a voice as Trundle crashed headlong into a pirate blundering about in the smoke. ''Ere! It's *you*!'

There was a dull swish and *thunk* noise and the pirate toppled over with a small arrow in him. Percy loaded his crossbow again as they ran on. Voices rose up all around them.

'They're getting away!'

'Stop 'em!'

Trundle followed Esmeralda's palm-light as they raced out of the Market Square and down a narrow side street. He risked a glance back. Beyond the houses, he could see the smoke swirling faster and faster as though it had been caught in a whirlwind. Then all the smoke went shooting up into the sky and vanished in a flash.

'Uh-oh!' said Esmeralda, looking back with worried eyes. 'That was Aunt Millie's magic, that was!'

'Keep running!' puffed Percy, the loaded crossbow in one hand, the big carpetbag in the other. 'We have to get to *The Thief in the Night* before they pull themselves together!'

'There they go!' croaked a raucous voice. Captain Slaughter was in the air like a black rag, his one eye gleaming with spite and vengefulness as he flapped towards them down the alley.

A *thwick!* sounded alongside Trundle's ear as a crossbow bolt zipped through the air.

'Awk!' screeched the raven as the bolt thudded into its wooden leg. 'Ark! Awrg! Yarook!' bawled the bird, as the added weight of the iron bolt sent it spiralling down to the cobbles in a feathery heap.

'Run!' hollered Percy.

'Get 'em!' roared the pirates.

'Urrrgh! Gruuurgh!' squawked the raven as several pairs of heavy pirates' boots trampled over him.

The three friends ran on, pelting through the streets of Port Shiverstones until they finally came to the docks. There was *The Iron Pig*, huge and ugly and rusting away, alongside one of the jetties, its red pirate flag flapping, its red sails furled.

Trundle and his friends hurtled along the jetty.
They could see their own trim little skyboat now!
They were almost there.

A riot of voices erupted behind them as
the first of the pirates came swarming out into the
docks.

The adventurers flung themselves into *The Thief
in the Night*. Esmeralda threw herself at the tiller.
Percy unfurled the sails. Trundle struggled for a
moment with the knots of the towrope. Losing
patience, he brought his sword down on the knot,
cutting the skyboat loose.

'All aboard who's coming aboard!' yelled
Esmeralda, yanking on the tiller. A moment later, the
skyboat pulled free of the jetty and went sailing up
into the sky. But even as they turned and drove into
a fresh tail wind, Trundle could see the hideous red

sails of *The Iron Pig* unrolling as the pirates raced back aboard.

They might have escaped for the moment – but their enemies would soon be hard on their heels.

The Land Beyond

'Any sign of pursuit, Trundle, my lad?' asked Percy.

'I thought I saw them a little while ago,' Trundle replied, peering through the long brass telescope. 'But I'm not so sure now.' There was a lot of dark cloud in their wake; *The Iron Pig* could be closing in on them, hidden in the rolling and threatening clouds.

Esmeralda had created a palm-light, by which Percy was examining the Crown of Stone.

'There's some writing inside the rim, just like I thought,' said Percy. 'It's in Badger Runes if I'm not mistaken.'

'Can you read them?' Trundle asked.

'Yes, indeed. I learned the old runes when I was a nipper.'

'Really?' Esmeralda said in surprise. 'I thought Badger Runes hadn't been used for thousands of years.'

'Well, you obviously thought wrong, my little friend,' Percy replied. He peered into the crown and began to recite in a slow, portentous voice.

Would you know where Sunsett lies?
Then seek you where day never dies.
Six crowns have you at journey's end

Place them on the stone altar, my good friend,

Then stand you ready – wonders for to see,

When the ancient powers at last be free!

'Well, well,' said Percy, resting the crown on his knees. 'Then Sunsett does still exist!'

'Hah!' chuckled Esmeralda. 'So much for all your science, Perce! It was there all along, and you lot at the Guild never knew it!'

'Indeed we did not,' the Herald admitted. 'But we still need to make sense of the rhyme. Sunsett is to be found where day never dies. Hmmmm.'

'That's just silly,' said Trundle. 'The day ends everywhere. I mean to say, you'd have to be on the wrong side of Nightreef to . . . be . . . where . . . the . . . day . . . never . . .' He became aware of Percy and Esmeralda staring at him. ' . . . dies . . .'

'The other side of Nightreef?' gasped

Esmeralda. 'But no
one lives there!'

'Don't they?'
asked Percy, his eyes
shining.

'*Do* they?'
breathed Esmeralda.

'I have no
idea,' said Percy. 'But I
think we should find out.'

'We're going to sail
sunwards beyond Nightreef?'
whispered Trundle. 'Oh,
my! Won't we get
burned to cinders?'

'Maybe we
will and maybe we
won't!' said

Esmeralda, with a toothy grin. 'Let's do it! Trun, drop the telescope and dig out the sky charts! We've a new course to navigate!'

'I don't understand why Aunt Millie wants the Six Crowns so bad that she's prepared to work with a bunch of putrid pirates,' said Esmeralda, as they sped through the starry darkness towards the huge black mass of Nightreef. 'What's it all about, Percy?'

'Well, there is an old, old story,' said Percy, 'concerning the Sect of the Sinister Spell.'

'Who are they?' asked Trundle. 'I've never heard of them.'

'Few people have,' said Percy, leaning forward as though sharing deep secrets. 'Did you know that the Badger Lords were served mostly by hedgehogs?' he asked.

'We kind of guessed that from the wind-galleon

that we found on Spyre,' said Esmeralda. 'Most of the crew were hedgehogs. They'd been turned to stone.'

'Well, the old tale says that there was a particularly intelligent and ambitious hedgehog called Grinder Prickleback,' said Percy. 'He saw no reason why the Badgers should have all the power. But they weren't interested in sharing their secrets, so Grinder brewed up a huge mind-control spell, hoping to use it to make the Badger Lords obey him. Unfortunately, something went horribly wrong with his spell – and the whole of the world was blown up!'

'Lawks!' gasped Trundle. 'So, the explosion that created the Sundered Lands was caused by a *hedgehog*?'

'So it would seem,' said Percy. 'But there's more. I've been reading some extremely old texts since you left the crowns with me, and I've found out some extraordinary things.' He gave them a sombre look.

'The Badgers got wind of what Grinder was up to, and just before the spell went wrong and everything was destroyed, they sent their six crowns out from Sunsett – scattering them far and wide.'

'But why didn't the Badgers save *themselves*?' asked Trundle.

'Most of their power resided in the crowns,' Percy explained. 'They stayed behind to try and defuse the spell. They failed of course, but they died in the hope that, one day, loyal hedgehogs might band together to gather the crowns and reunite the shattered fragments of the world.'

'Which is why they hid the clues along with the crowns,' said Esmeralda. 'I get it! But what has this to do with Aunt Millie?'

'I believe she may be a member of the Sect of the Sinister Spell,' explained Percy. 'An ancient, secret society, whose aim is to bring the crowns together and use their power to re-cast Grinder Prickleback's spell!'

'Why would they do that?' asked Trundle.

'In the hope that they can use it to bring all of the Sundered Lands under their sway!' pronounced the Herald. 'I believe that is why Esmeralda's aunt is so intent on getting her hands on the crowns! She's going to use their powers to brew up the spell again so she can control the mind of every person living in the Sundered Lands!'

Trundle eyed the Herald Persuivant in alarm. 'Then we really *must* stop her,' he gulped, horrified by Millie Rose Thorne's evil ambition.

'Indeed, we must!' agreed Percy. 'For everyone's sake!'

'Nightreef ho!' called Esmeralda from the tiller.

Trundle lifted his snout and gazed ahead of them. They were so close to Nightreef that it filled half the sky, blotting out the stars. It was black and featureless, and so huge that it made Trundle feel that he and *The Thief in the Night* and everyone else aboard were no bigger than gnats.

Esmeralda shifted their course, catching the rushing winds so that the gallant little skyboat rose higher and higher across the black mass of the reef, tacking to and fro while every moment more stars vanished and the oppressive blackness loomed closer and closer, like a vast gaping mouth waiting to swallow them up.

Trundle cowered in the bows as Nightreef rushed closer. He hardly dared to look at it. No one spoke. Even Esmeralda didn't seem to have anything to say. And as the monstrous darkness hurtled at them, Trundle became quite convinced that Nightreef had no end – that they would be engulfed by its blackness and lost for ever.

But then he noticed a glimmer above them – a thin silvery line of light, as thrilling and exciting as a new dawn. They raced on towards the thread of light. It came closer and closer, and grew wider and brighter and longer and deeper.

Then, with a whoop from Esmeralda, *The Thief in the Night* lifted above the long whaleback of Nightreef and came shooting into dazzling sunlight. The sky was blue – a fierce, blazing blue that was like diamonds and sapphires.

Trundle rubbed his eyes, blinded for a few moments by the intense light.

'Don't risk looking into the sun,' warned Percy. 'Shield your eyes! But *look*!'

Trundle peeped from between his fingers. Ahead of them, across a short space of gleaming crystal air, he saw an island.

'Sunsett!' breathed Trundle. 'Well I never!'

Sunsett! The home of the Ancient Badger Lords.

As they sailed closer, it struck Trundle as a beautiful but desolate place. It was hard to imagine anything being alive here. It was a landscape of sun-bleached cliffs and white stony valleys, of barren rocky deserts and undulating sand dunes, stretching as far as the eye could see, baked hard and dry by the merciless stare of the unsleeping sun.

Not a bird clove the air. Not a blade of grass poked itself out of the ground.

'What a dreadful place!' murmured Esmeralda. 'There's nothing here. Nothing at all.'

'There must be,' said Percy. 'I'm sure of it.'

'Face it, Perce, if there ever was anything here, it would have crumbled to dust by now. I don't think anything could survive in this heat!'

'What's that?' asked Trundle, pointing to a

sharp ridge of land at
the end of a long
narrow valley.

'A bunch
of old rocks!'
grumbled
Esmeralda.

But Trundle
wasn't so sure. He grabbed up the telescope and
applied it to his eye. A towering cliff-face of brown
stone leaped forward.

'There are carvings on it!' he gasped. 'Fantastic
carvings!'

It wasn't long before they could all see what
Trundle had seen. Etched deep into the rock was the
front wall of a great palace or temple. Huge stone steps
led to a deep entranceway flanked by tall pillars.

'It looks like something has survived after all!'

said Percy, his voice quivering with excitement. 'Bring us down, Esmeralda. And let's hope that doorway leads somewhere!'

'I bet it will!' said Trundle. 'I bet it will lead us somewhere amazing!'

Esmeralda brought *The Thief in the Night* down to a smooth, gliding landing that cut a narrow furrow in the sand only a few metres away from the huge dark entranceway carved into the cliff.

The three adventurers disembarked and plodded through the fine, shimmering sand. Percy left the carpetbag behind, the crossbow and quiver now slung over his shoulder. Trundle carried the Dwindling Box in a backpack, all six crowns stowed safely within.

They climbed the steps and walked cautiously into the darkness of the deep entrance. There was no doorway, although they saw the remains of hinges that suggested that once, long ago, there had been

immense, heavy doors guarding the way in.

They walked down a long, square tunnel that stretched away into cool darkness. Esmeralda conjured up a palm-light so they could see where they were going. The walls and ceiling of the tunnel were smooth and featureless, and there was a fine layer of sand underfoot, blown in by the wind.

Trundle glanced over his shoulder, seeing their three sets of footprints winding back to the bright square of the entrance. *No one has been here for thousands upon thousands of years*, he thought to himself. The idea struck him as sad and a little bit creepy.

Esmeralda stopped, lifting her snout and sniffing.

'What is it?' asked Percy.

'I smell magic!' she said, her voice echoing back and forth between the thick stone walls. 'Very old magic, I'd say! We'd better be prepared for unexpected things to happen.'

'What kind of things?' asked Trundle with a shudder.

Esmeralda eyed him. 'If I knew that, they wouldn't be unexpected now, would they?' she said.

'I suppose not,' Trundle had to admit.

'Our purpose here is to find the altar mentioned in the rhyme,' said Percy. 'Let's keep our eyes peeled!'

They marched on, Esmeralda in the lead, Percy close behind, and Trundle bringing up the rear. And that was why it was Trundle who first heard the noises behind them.

He turned, staring back the way they had come. The sounds had been very faint and far off, but they rang unpleasant bells in his head. He held his breath and listened intently. There was creaking – like windship timbers – and a swooshing sound like wind in sails. And then there was a long, sliding crunch . . . as of something large coming in to land in the sand.

'Hold on a moment,' he said.

'What is it, my boy?' asked Percy, coming back to his side.

'Something has just arrived,' Trundle said with a gulp.

'Pirates?' breathed Esmeralda.

'Who else?' said Percy.

And even as they stood there, hollow, booming voices came echoing down the tunnel. Trundle couldn't make any sense of what was being said, but the voices were cruel and harsh. And then, black shapes began to appear in the square of hot golden light at the entrance to the tunnel.

'Rats!' hissed Esmeralda. 'That's Grizzletusk's scurvy crew for sure! I'd hoped we'd outrun 'em!'

'Perhaps we still can,' said Percy. 'Come along

– swift's the word, my young friends! Swift's the word!' And so saying, Percy began to trot along the corridor at a surprising speed.

Esmeralda and Trundle looked at one another for a moment, then chased after him.

Maybe he was right – maybe they could outrun Grizzletusk and his murderous band of cut-throats – but Trundle couldn't help but feel they were doing no more than running deeper and deeper into a trap from which there could be no escape.

Hearth and Home

'Oh, great,' groaned Esmeralda, holding up her palm-light. 'Can anyone swim at all?'

'Not as such,' said Trundle.

'I've never tried,' added Percy.

'Me neither,' said Esmeralda. 'Which means we have a bit of a problem.'

The three of them gazed out over a wide lake of

112

dark water that stretched from one wall of the tunnel to the other, entirely blocking their way ahead. The still, murky water was dotted with large, pale blobby things that looked like a cross between lily pads and mushrooms.

'It might be shallow,' suggested Trundle, drawing his sword and kneeling at the brink of the lake. He lowered the blade into the water, hoping for its point to touch the bottom. It didn't.

'Maybe we could jump from pad to pad?' he suggested.

'I think we have to risk it,' said Percy. 'Listen!'

The tunnel reverberated with shouting and with running feet. The pirates weren't far behind, and the longer they stood there wondering what to do, the closer Grizzletusk's bloodthirsty hoards would come.

'It's got my vote!' said Esmeralda. 'Here goes!' She backed up a few paces then ran for the brimming brink of the lake. Trundle could hardly watch as she sailed through the air. But she landed safely. The pad wobbled and drifted a little, but she kept her footing.

She paused for a few moments, then made a second jump on to the nearest pad. The puffy growth tilted and she had to stop to adjust her balance. Ripples spread across the lake and lapped the banks.

She grinned back. 'It's fun!' she shouted. 'Come on!' She took another flying leap and then another and suddenly she was halfway across the lake.

Percy took a deep breath and made the first leap. 'Woo-hoop!' he gasped, his

114

arms flapping as he fought for balance. But then he steadied himself and took the next leap.

Trundle wasn't a big fan of deep water. But even if he fell in, the pads were close enough together for him to splash his way to one of them and climb aboard. He hoped!

He took a breath and jumped. The pad was unpleasantly squishy and wobbly under his feet, like a worn-out and soggy old mattress. But he kept his balance easily enough and flung himself forward on to the next pad.

'Get a move on, slowcoaches!' yelled Esmeralda. She was full of confidence now, trampolining her way from pad to pad, and almost at the far side of the lake.

'Be careful!' warned Percy.

'Oh, please!' retorted Esmeralda. 'As if I'd—whoops!' Her overconfidence let her down. Her foot slipped on one of the pads and she went slithering feet first over the edge.

Trundle was about to yell at her for showing off, when something struck him. There had been no splash!

Esmeralda was clinging grimly to the far side of the pad, her eyes full of fear.

'There's no water!' she gasped, clawing at the mushy pad.

'What do you mean?' called Percy.

'I'm hanging in . . . *nothing*!' yelled Esmeralda. 'This isn't a lake!' She called out loudly. 'Magic be gone! Truth be revealed!'

Trundle felt an odd sensation, like an icy wind rushing into his eyes – and suddenly everything around him looked different.

'Lawks!' he wailed, staring down into a great deep dark chasm. The water had vanished away and the blobby pads had turned into chunks of floating powerstone. And worst of all was the fact that evil greedy eyes were peering up at them from the black depths.

And even as Trundle stared in horror into the chasm, the powerstone shifted under his feet and he lost his balance and fell. He just managed to snatch hold of the edge of the bobbing powerstone rock. He hung there, gasping for breath, his legs dangling.

'Hold steady there, both of you!' called Percy. 'Trundle, I'm coming!'

Trundle hung on grimly as Percy unwound the rope belt from around his waist. He swung twice then let the end of the rope snake out towards Trundle.

The rope flicked past Trundle's snout. He made a frantic grab for it and caught it in both hands. For a few dire moments, Trundle hung in the chasm, clinging on grimly to the rope as Percy hauled hard on the other end. He was sure he heard champing jaws below him, but a few good strong pulls from Percy and he was soon safe aboard the floating chunk of powerstone.

'Thank you!' he panted. 'There are things down there – creatures!'

'It's probably best not to look down,' Percy suggested.

'I'm still hanging here, when you're ready!' called Esmeralda. 'No hurry – take your time!'

'We're coming, Esmeralda,' Percy said.

'So are the pirates!' yelped Trundle. Some way back along the tunnel, the red light of torches could now be seen, accompanied by shouting voices and stamping feet.

Hand in hand, Trundle and Percy began to leap towards Esmeralda. Trundle tried not to think of the hungry beasts that were lurking below, waiting for a tasty meal to drop into their mouths.

They reached Esmeralda and hauled her to safety.

'There they are!' howled Grizzletusk. 'On the other side of the lake! Dive in, me hearties! Go get 'em!'

Excellent! thought Trundle. *They still see the water! This should be interesting.*

It was. A few of the pirates leaped into the non-existent water and went wailing down into the depths. Slavering and chewing noises sounded from the deep darkness.

'Stop, you fools!' shouted Millie Rose Thorne. 'It's not real. The water is an illusion! Can't you see that? Shoot them!'

'Muskets up, lads!' bellowed Razorback. 'Fill 'em with holes!'

'Let's get going!' said Esmeralda as several pirates fired at once.

Trundle and Percy didn't need telling twice. With three long bounds, they reached the far side of the chasm, bullets and balls whistling around their ears.

As they pelted along the tunnel, Trundle looked back. The pirates were crossing the chasm, jumping from stone to stone. He was rather pleased to see that a few of them lost their footing and plunged into the chasm.

The beasts down there were going to have quite a feast!

It felt to Trundle as though they'd been running along this slowly descending tunnel for ever.

'Must pause . . . for breath . . .' he gasped.

'No time!' exclaimed Esmeralda. 'Do you want the pirates to catch us?'

'No . . . but . . .'

'Look!' Percy said, pointing up ahead to where

a stone door hung open. 'We're reached somewhere at last!'

'See, Trun?' said Esmeralda. 'Buck up, there's a good fellow.'

Trundle gathered his last remaining strength and tottered towards the doorway.

They entered into a gaping darkness. Esmeralda muttered something and her palm-light grew brighter. They had come into a long room lined with tall, carved wooden caskets standing on end. Some of the caskets were broken open, revealing the upright mummified remains of animals. But the caskets didn't only contain mummies – there was treasure as well. Sparkling rings spilled out over the sandy floor, along with coins and necklaces and bracelets and jewels.

'Oooh!' breathed Esmeralda, reaching for a silver tiara. 'Pretty things!'

'No!' barked Percy. 'Trust me! Touch nothing –

let's get out of here before anything happens.'

'Like what?' asked Trundle, gazing spellbound at all the beautiful things strewn so enticingly over the ground.

'I don't know,' said Percy. 'But look at that!' He pointed to something huddled in a corner. It was a skeleton, shrouded in faded rags. And now Trundle looked more carefully, he saw that there were several other skeletons sprawled on the ground.

'Do you think they were trying to steal the treasure?' asked Esmeralda.

'Yes,' Percy replied.

'So . . . what killed them?' asked Trundle.

'I don't know,' said Percy. 'That's what worries me.'

'He's right, let's get out of here!' agreed Esmeralda.

They trotted the length of the chamber. Trundle

counted at least a dozen skeletons before they came to an arched doorway at the far end.

'Maybe we could shift some of these mummy cases to block the way out?' Esmeralda suggested. 'It'll slow the pirates down.'

The wooden cases were heavy and unwieldy, but they did manage to drag a couple from their niches in the walls and tip them over across the doorway. They were about to shove a third casket into place when they heard voices from the other end of the chamber.

They scrambled wildly over the barricade of caskets as the pirates came pouring into the long room.

'Cor!' they heard one of the pirates say. 'Take a gander at all this treasure, mateys!'

'Loads and loads of jools!' hollered another. 'Enough to retire on!'

'Why bother chasing them hedgehogs when

there's all this luvvery loot just lyin' around for the takin'?' suggested yet another.

Trundle peeped over the top of the barrier. In the flickering torchlight, he saw the pirates milling around, grabbing up handfuls of jewellery and trinkets.

'You're right there, me buckos,' growled Razorback, snatching up a fistful of coins. 'I says we snaffle what we can and head back to *The Iron Pig*!'

'Not on your slippery guts, you don't!' snarled Grizzletusk, barging his way into the chamber. 'We can take our pick of this stuff on the way back. Meanwhile – get after them hedgehogs. Smart, now!'

There was some grumbling at this.

'You fools!' shouted Millie Rose Thorne, coming into the room behind the captain. 'You call this treasure? It's nothing compared with what you'll get once we have those three hedgehogs in our clutches!'

'Maybe so,' muttered Razorback, 'but I'm not

leaving here empty-handed!' And so saying, he shoved
the fistful of coins into a pocket.

'Grrrrwwwwwwwwllllll!' A long deep, eerie
snarling sound rang through the chamber.
'Grahhhhhhh-rrrrgggghhhh!'

Trundle
watched in
mute dread as
the mummies in
the open caskets
began to twitch and
writhe. Their eyes
opened, revealing
an eerie light.

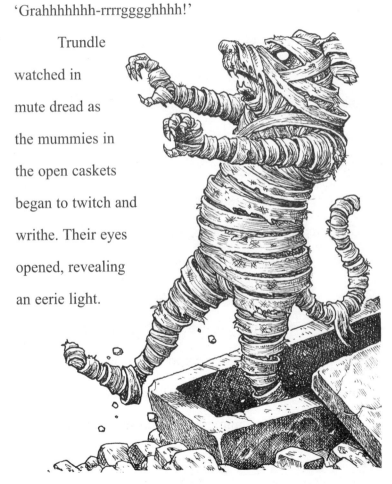

Their arms lifted, fingers curling like claws – and then
– horror of horrors! – they came lurching out of their
caskets on stiff and jerky legs.

'Oh, lummy!' shrieked one of the pirates.
'Mummies!'

'They're alive!' howled another.

'Have your money back!' yelled Razorback,
throwing the coins at the mummies as they loomed up
in their rotted and ragged old bandages. 'I don't want
none of it!'

'Too late!' intoned the mummies, as they
shambled forward. 'Come! Join us in our tombs! Stay
with us for ever!'

The terrified pirates scattered in all directions as
the long bony fingers of the mummies reached for their
throats. A few guns went off, spouting smoke. But the
shots went straight through the musty old bandages,
and judging from their snarls and from the hideous

light burning in their empty eye sockets, being shot at only made the mummies angrier.

'Let's get out of here,' breathed Esmeralda, at Trundle's shoulder. 'Those mummies might not be too fussy who they attack next!'

Even as she spoke, the lid of one of the caskets they had tipped over in front of the door flew open and a withered and bandaged arm reached up, bony fingers snatching for Trundle's throat.

He whipped his sword out and struck at the clutching hand, severing it at the wrist so it plopped down into the sand. But the hand just reared up on its fingers and came scuttling after Trundle like some dreadful spider-thing.

Even a bolt from Percy's crossbow didn't slow the horrid thing down. Biting his lip in terror, Trundle whacked at the hand with the flat of his blade. *Whack! Whacketty-whack!*

'I think you got it, Trun,' Esmeralda said, prodding the crushed hand with her toe.

'Are you sure?' stammered Trundle.

'I'd say so!' Esmeralda replied. 'And now, we'd better make ourselves scarce!'

The three friends ran again, the yelling and wailing of the belaboured pirates following them along the tunnel.

'Perhaps they'll all be killed?' Trundle ventured hopefully.

'Don't bet on it!' panted Esmeralda. 'My aunt Millie is back there, too. I think she has magic enough to deal with a few mummies.'

This new tunnel was quite different from the previous one. It descended steeply, winding around and around itself like a corkscrew until, quite suddenly, it split in two, each fork blocked by a wooden door.

'Now what?' wondered Trundle. 'Which way do we go?'

'The chances are that one way will lead us on, and the other will be a terrible trap!' said Percy.

'Look at this,' said Esmeralda. Carved low into the wall at the very place the tunnel divided were some words, half hidden by drifting sand.

Percy stooped and brushed the sand aside, revealing more words.

Beware, beware, the sinister path
The other leads to home and hearth

'What does that mean?' asked Esmeralda. 'Which path is which?'

'Sinister used to mean "left",' said Percy.

'So we should follow the right-hand tunnel?' said Trundle. 'Home and hearth sound good to me!'

He cocked his ears. 'Can you hear that?'

The sounds of pursuit could be heard again – not terribly close yet, but not far enough away either.

'I was right,' said Esmeralda. 'Some of them must have got away from the mummies.' She looked at Percy. 'But can we trust this clue, Perce?' she asked. 'Isn't it a wee bit too convenient?'

'I don't care about that!' said Trundle. 'Whatever is ahead, it can't be worse than what's behind!' And so saying, he turned the handle of the right-hand door and stepped through.

'My word, it's nice to be home,' Trundle said, closing his front door behind himself and resting his lamplighting pole against the wall. He sniffed the appetizing scent of cabbage broth. 'Just what I need at the end of a busy evening lighting the lamps of Port Shiverstones.'

Rubbing his hands together, he headed for his small kitchen, looking forward to nothing more energetic than a quiet evening with his snout in a good book.

Of the Badger Lords of Old and the six lost crowns, of Esmeralda Lightfoot and the Herald Persuivant, of Millie Rose Thorne and Captain Grizzletusk's pirates, he remembered not the smallest thing!

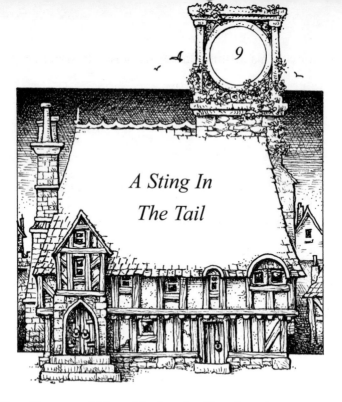

9

A Sting In The Tail

Trundle poured himself a bowl of broth and sat down in his comfy armchair by the fire. He picked up *The Book of Unbelievable Jaunts and Escapades*, and opened it where he had left off the previous evening.

    Chapter Seven. The Extraordinary Adventure of Gruffly Grimm and the Swampy Thing.

    He did enjoy a good adventure – and Gruffly

Grimm was his all-time favourite hero. He sighed as he settled down to read, a small part of him wishing he could be a brave and bold adventurer like Gruffly.

Knock!

He frowned, glancing towards the door. Who could that be, disturbing him at this time of night?

Knock! Knock!

'I bet it's those Stubbleberry twins, playing knock-and-run!' he grumbled. 'They're always up to mischief, those two!'

Knock-knock-knock-knock-knock!!

A positive fusillade of knocks resounded on the outside of his door. Putting his book down,

Trundle marched across his small living room. He could hear unfamiliar voices shouting from outside the door. A male voice and a female voice.

'Trundle! Let us in! The pirates are coming! Open up!'

'Go away!' Trundle called crossly. 'Pirates, indeed! In Port Shiverstones! What nonsense!'

The knocking started up again with renewed vigour, until his poor front door was shaking from the assault.

'I've had enough of this!' Trundle declared, snatching the door open and intending to give the noisy visitors a piece of his mind. 'Now, look here . . .' Two hedgehogs stood on his doorstep – a middle-aged fellow in robes, and a young female with a ferocious expression.

'You prize idiot, Trundle!' yelled the girl. 'What's the idea of— oh!' She stared beyond Trundle.

'Oh! Lawks! Percy – it's a magic room! It's the spitting image of his living room in Port Shiverstones. We have to get him out of there!'

'Now just you hold on a moment,' cried Trundle as two pairs of hands grabbed at him. 'If you think you can just turn up and— awk!' He was dragged bodily across the threshold and the door was slammed shut at his back.

Trundle sat in the sandy tunnel, staring around himself in shock and amazement.

'Jimminy!' he gasped. 'I thought I was back home! I forgot everything! What happened?'

'Magic happened,' Esmeralda declared, helping him to his feet. 'Didn't I tell you to be prepared for the unexpected?'

'Well, yes,' Trundle admitted. 'But the problem with that is—'

'Pirates!' warned Percy. 'Getting closer!'

'The left-hand door it is, then!' said Esmeralda. 'Lead on, Percy!'

Percy threw the other door open and they all piled through, Trundle still feeling rather foolish to have been so easily deceived by the magic room.

They slammed the door and went pelting along the new tunnel as fast as their legs would take them.

The tunnel rose steeply, getting narrower and narrower until they had to move in single file. But then, quite suddenly and startlingly, it opened up and they found themselves gazing down into a huge round chamber stuffed solid with a dazzling confusion of golden treasures.

There were golden statues and sarcophagi, there were golden thrones, and golden tables laden with golden goblets and plates and bowls. There were golden caskets and coffers and chests, and golden trinkets and ornaments and baubles. And the glorious treasures were all jumbled together in the cavern as though they had been thrown in there and forgotten.

The tunnel had brought them to a lofty gallery, far above the teeming golden hoard. Blinking in wonderment and awe, they climbed down a flight of stone steps.

'Such wealth!' breathed Percy as they wound their way between the towering golden treasures. 'Such beautiful things!'

'But is the altar in here?' Esmeralda wondered.

'I don't think it is,' said Percy. 'The rhyme said the altar was made of stone – but everything in here is of gold.' He pointed to where another flight of stone steps zigzagged up to a dark hole in the far wall of the cavern. 'I think we need to go up there and hope for the best.'

They were right at the top of the winding stairway when a bloom of red torchlight appeared on the far side of the cavern. The pirates had arrived.

Quick as a flash, Esmeralda brought her hand down on her palm-light, plunging the three of them into darkness. 'Shhh!' she hissed. 'Let's see how many of them are left.'

Grizzletusk was in the lead, carrying a flaring torch. Trundle saw the greed ignite in his eyes as he stared down at the gleaming treasure trove. He went stomping down the stairs, the torch held high. There were a lot of 'ooohs' and 'ahhhs' and 'luvaducks' as the pirates that came after him caught sight of the wonderful confusion of golden objects.

Only Aunt Millie seemed indifferent to the wealth on display, as she plodded grimly down the stone steps with her raven on her shoulder.

The pirates spread out among the treasures, fingering them and stroking them.

'Watch out for mummies!' someone warned.

'There are no mummies here, me hearties,' said Razorback. He gave Captain Grizzletusk a hard look. 'I says enough is enough!' he growled. 'I vote we forget them there crowns and concentrate on making ourselves rich!'

'You mutinous hog!' growled Grizzletusk. 'I make the decisions around here, and I say we get them crowns first, then come back for this lot afterwards!'

'Sez you!' snarled Razorback.

'Yeah, sez me!' roared Grizzletusk, aiming his pistol at the glowering bo'sun.

A moment later, and Razorback's own gun was out and levelled at his brutish leader. The other pirates became silent, watching the two huge hogs as they faced off.

Wouldn't that be perfect? Trundle thought to himself. *If they had a falling-out and all killed one another!*

But before anything more could be said, Millie Rose Thorne stepped between the two hogs. 'Idiots!' she shouted, glaring at the protagonists. 'Cut out the nonsense! We have work to do!' A dangerous light glittered in her eyes. She lifted her hands and black threads began to spin out from her fingers. 'Or do I have to show you who's really the boss here?'

Grizzletusk and Razorback lowered their weapons, and a relieved sigh went through the other pirates.

'She's the boss!' croaked her raven, launching itself from her shoulder and flapping heavily over to a large casket topped off with a statue of a golden scorpion. The raven came down to perch on the scorpion's glittering head. 'Crowns first! Booty later!' it croaked. 'That's the way to do it!'

As the heavy black bird settled on the head of the golden scorpion, Trundle became aware of a whirring and clicking and clunking sound, as if some kind of machinery was grinding slowly into action.

'Strike me pink!' screeched the raven, leaping into the air as the casket under him split slowly into two halves. There were more clanking noises, and a moment later, a large, rusty iron claw emerged from the open casket and snapped at the raven. There was a loud squawk and suddenly there was no raven any more and the air was full of black feathers.

'What in the Sundered Lands is that?' murmured Percy.

The pirates nearest to the cracked-open casket backed off nervously as a large shape heaved itself out into the torchlight.

It was a monstrous scorpion – but a scorpion made entirely of rusty iron! It moved with slow clanking purpose, its claws opening and closing and its curved tail lifted high above its body.

'Kill it!' roared Grizzletusk, firing his own pistol at the looming monster.

There was a lot of yelling and shooting and billowing smoke and coughing and choking – but when the gun smoke cleared, the scorpion was still there, not in the least bit damaged – and it had a limp pirate in each claw.

'Run for it!' someone howled, and the pirates scattered. But the great clanking and whirring scorpion leaped forward with startling speed, and *snap! snap!* two more pirates lay dead.

Millie Rose Thorne held her ground, her hands reaching out towards the monstrous mechanical device, threads of black spinning out from her fingertips.

The long, segmented tail of the scorpion struck out, the barbed stinger cutting through Millie's mystical webs like a sword through string.

'My magic threads!' screeched Aunt Millie. 'Ruined!'

'Arrrgh!' howled the pirates, falling over one another as they made a frantic scramble for the stairway out. 'Gangway! Help! Arrgh!'

'We'd better get going,' mumbled Esmeralda from their high perch. 'I think this is going to get nasty!'

Trundle didn't need a second telling. The great iron monster was springing and leaping this way and that among the fleeing pirates, its sting stabbing down, its claws clashing. He saw the sting stab into Grizzletusk's back as he tried to escape. He saw Razorback trampling his comrades as he made a wild but futile run for the stairs.

Esmeralda ignited a palm-light and the three friends turned away from the gruesome carnage and headed into the tunnel that led from the top of the stairs.

'Well, I guess they got theirs,' said Esmeralda as

they tried as quickly as possible to get out of earshot of the grim and grisly goings-on in the golden chamber. 'I can't help feeling sorry for poor old Aunt Millie, though – what a way to go!'

She stopped in her tracks. 'What am I saying?' she gasped. 'This whole business was her fault! Good riddance, I say!'

Trundle couldn't help but agree. All the same, being chopped into confetti by a gigantic iron scorpion was a pretty awful way to go!

'Ahh!' breathed Percy. 'I think we've come to journey's end at last!'

They were only a few minutes out from the golden chamber, standing at the curved entranceway to a small domed room. It was quite empty and plain, save for a six-sided block of white stone that stood in the middle of the floor.

Trundle's fingers and toes and whiskers were prickling, as if there was something different in the air of this little round room.

'This must be the stone altar in the rhyme,' whispered Esmeralda. Even she seemed to understand that this was a special place where it would be wrong to use loud voices.

'I do believe it is,' said Percy, tiptoeing into the room. 'The stone altar of the Badger Lords. I never thought I'd live to see it!'

They stepped quietly across the floor and walked around the altar. On its six sides were depicted carvings of six badgers, each surrounded by bowing or kneeling hedgehogs, and each one with a different crown on his head. Above each side, a hollow had been cut into the top of the altar – six hollows into which, Trundle guessed, the six crowns would fit, neat as neat. In the very centre of the altar, Trundle noticed a small, deep slot.

'I wonder what that's for,' he said.

'Who knows?' murmured Esmeralda. 'Come on, Trun – get the crowns out – I'm dying to see what happens next!'

Trundle retrieved the Dwindling Box from his backpack. He unlatched the lid and, kneeling on the ground, he tilted the box and shook it gently. The Crown of Wood came rolling out, tiny at first, but quickly growing to its full size.

Esmeralda picked it up and popped it in the hollow above the picture of the Badger Lord wearing the same crown.

Meanwhile Trundle gave the box another little shake and the Crown of Ice rolled out and grew. Percy retrieved it and put it in its place.

But just as Trundle was about to give the box a third shake, a ragged and grim-faced apparition appeared at the entrance, her headscarf in tatters, her prickles battered and bent and her dress cut all to ribbons.

'Step away from the crowns,' she growled. 'And quick about it!'

Millie Rose Thorne held a pistol in each paw, and she looked in just the right mood to use them.

10

The Crowns Of Power

'How did you get away from the scorpion, Aunty?'
Esmeralda asked warily as Millie Rose Thorne limped
into the chamber. 'I bet you had to use up a whole lot
of magic to escape,' she said. 'In fact, I'd guess you're
all magicked-out right now.'

'You're quite right, my dear,' said her aunt. 'But
I don't need magic to deal with you three – not when I

have two primed and loaded pistols. Now, get away from that box.'

The three companions backed away from the altar, leaving the Dwindling Box lying on its side on the ground.

'Did any of the pirates survive?' Trundle asked.

'I doubt that very much,' said Aunt Millie. 'But they did what I needed them to do. They got me to this place.' She gestured towards Esmeralda with one of the pistols. 'Now then, my dear, I need you to take the rest of the crowns out of that remarkable box and place them on the altar.'

'Not on your nelly!' snapped Esmeralda. 'I'm not doing your dirty work for you!'

Aunt Millie levelled a pistol at Trundle. 'You have to the count of three, then I shoot your witless little friend!' she snarled.

'Hey, less of the witless,' said Trundle.

'All right,' Esmeralda said quickly. 'I get it! The loony aunt has the guns, everyone has to obey her.' Muttering under her breath things that Trundle guessed her aunt was better off not hearing, Esmeralda went to the Dwindling Box.

Suddenly, she shouted some strange words and flung her arm out towards her aunt. A ball of lightning whizzed through the air. Millie Rose Thorne blew at the hissing ball, like someone puffing out a candle. The lightning fizzled away and vanished.

'Oh, rats!' groaned Esmeralda, wringing her stinging hand.

'Try that again and fattie dies!' snarled her aunt.

'Fattie?' gasped Trundle. 'Now, look here . . .'

'Shush, Trun!' said Esmeralda. 'We have to do what she wants.' She looked at her aunt. 'I know what you're up to, Aunty,' she said. 'We know all about the Sect of the Sinister Spell.'

'Do you, indeed?' chuckled Aunt Millie. 'Who's a clever girl, then?'

'You'll never get away with this!' added Trundle.

'Who's going to stop me?' asked Aunt Millie. 'You three? I think not!'

Trundle noticed a movement in the tunnel behind the Roamany Queen. Something large was looming up towards her, moving slowly and stealthily.

'Look behind you, Millie!' said Percy, peering at the same big shadowy thing that had taken Trundle's attention. 'I think we have a visitor.'

'You're not going to fool me with that old trick, Grinder!' Millie cackled. 'Just how silly do you think I am?'

At that moment, a clank and a whirr sounded from the tunnel.

'Pretty silly, actually,' said Esmeralda.

Millie was about to say something when a huge, rusted iron stinger came darting out of the darkness of the tunnel. It struck her in the neck and she went as stiff as a board, the two pistols falling from her fingers.

'Drat the thing!' she hissed between gritted teeth. 'Esmeralda, this is all your fault! I'll get you for this, you see if—' The tail of the mechanical scorpion wrapped around Aunt Millie's waist and she was whipped away into the tunnel before she could say another word.

Esmeralda stared after her with a shocked look on her face.

'Do you think that's the last we'll see of her?' she murmured.

'I think so,' said Percy.

But Trundle had other concerns on his mind right then. He turned to Percy, a puzzled look on his brow. 'You two know each other,' he said.

'What do you mean, Trundle, my boy?' asked Percy.

'You just called her Millie and she called you . . . well . . . she called you *Grinder*,' said Trundle. 'As in Grinder Prickleback – the hedgehog who blew the world up thousands of years ago.'

'That she did!' gasped Esmeralda, glaring at the Herald Persuivant. 'What's going on, Percy – if that's your real name at all! How come my aunt called you Grinder – and how do you two know each other?'

'Well, aren't you the pair of clever-clogs!' said Percy with a wide smile. 'You're quite right, of course, we do know one another. But we're members of quite different branches of the Sect of the Sinister Spell.'

'Are you some kind of descendant of the original Grinder Prickleback?' demanded Esmeralda. 'Is that why you have the same name?'

Percy chuckled, waggling a finger at them.

'No,' he said. 'I'm not a *descendant* of Grinder Prickleback.' He slipped his crossbow from his shoulder and quickly armed it with one of the deadly metal darts. 'I *am* Grinder Prickleback.'

'No way!' breathed Esmeralda.

Percy laughed. 'I am rather well preserved for my age,' he said. 'I spoke the Vile Rune of Neverending Life.' His eyebrows lowered threateningly. 'And then I waited for someone to come along who would be able to find the crowns and bring me here. My, how I waited! Years became decades, decades became centuries – centuries became millennia. And still I waited . . . and finally, after two thousand years, the pair of you turned up and I knew my time had come at last!'

'Talk about *patient*,' gasped Trundle. 'But what was the plan? Why did you want to come back here?'

'Why, to brew my great spell again!' said Percy.

'But this time it won't go wrong – and this time I shall use it to bring the whole of the Sundered Lands under my control.'

'You treacherous traitor!' gasped Trundle. 'And to think we trusted you!'

'Hmm, that was probably a mistake, Trundle, my lad,' said Percy, edging around the chamber and stooping to pick up Millie's pistols. One he tucked into his belt, the other he pointed towards them. 'Come along now – chop chop! Those crowns won't put themselves on the altar, now, will they?' He smiled a friendly smile. 'And don't try any of your feeble magic on me, Esmeralda – or someone is going to get hurt.'

'Wretch!' growled Esmeralda. 'Cowardly stinker!'

'The crowns, if you please!' snapped Percy, waving the crossbow and the pistol at them.

'But if you're Grinder Prickleback, how is it

you didn't know about all the traps and tricks down here?' asked Trundle. 'You've been behaving as if you've never seen this place before.'

Percy's eyes narrowed nastily. 'Us hedgehogs were never allowed into the Badgers' inner sanctum,' he growled. 'We weren't good enough for that! Those uppity Badger Lords never really trusted us with their big secrets.'

'Can you blame them?' asked Trundle. 'I mean to say!'

'No more chatting!' said Percy. 'Get busy!'

Deeply miserable and totally deflated, Trundle tipped the Dwindling Box so that the rest of the crowns came rolling out.

To think that Percy of all people was a villain! And a two-thousand-year-old villain at that! Trundle gave an inner groan. How could they have been so completely fooled?

Soon, all six of the crowns were in their places on the white stone altar. Trundle and Esmeralda stepped back, wondering what would happen next. Despite the six crowns being so close to one another, there was no vibrating or buzzing, no blue lightning, no sign of magic at all!

'Excellent!' said Percy. 'Now for the final act!' He clambered on to the top of the altar. He stood there for a few moments, as though catching his breath, then he lifted his snout to the roof and spoke in a loud, commanding voice.

'Crowns of the Badger Lords, awaken!'

There was a long silent pause.

Percy cleared his throat and called out again, 'Crowns of the Badger Lords! Awaken!'

Nothing happened.

'Uh, Perce?' said Esmeralda. 'I don't think the crowns can hear you.'

'Oi!' exclaimed Trundle as his sword began to vibrate wildly in his belt. 'I'm being shooken to bits!' The sword thrashed frantically to and fro, as though desperate to get free. 'Wha-wha-what's gug-gug-going on?'

Percy stared at him. 'The sword!' he shouted. He stared down between his feet at the narrow slot cut into the top of the altar. 'It fits in here! I should have guessed. The sword is the final piece needed to activate the crowns! Give it to me, Trundle! Give it to me now!'

'Shan't!' declared Trundle, grabbing the hilt of his shaking sword in both paws. 'Shoot me if you like! I refuse to give it to you!'

Percy aimed both the pistol and the crossbow at Trundle.

Esmeralda jumped between them, her paws in the air. 'Don't shoot!' she shouted. 'Trundle – give the sword to him – he'll regret it, I promise you!'

Trundle looked at her. 'Really?'

'Really,' she replied. 'Trust me.'

Reluctantly, Trundle stepped up to the altar. He drew the struggling sword from his belt and handed it up to Percy.

A wide grin stretched over Percy's snout. 'A wise choice, my boy,' he said.

'Speaking of wise choices,' said Esmeralda. 'Listen to me, Percy . . . or Grinder, or whatever your name is. I'm a Roamany, I am. I may not be big on nasty spells like my aunt, but I have the sixth sense. And I'm telling you, pal, if you put that sword into that slot, you'll regret it!'

Percy raised an eyebrow. 'Yes, well, as much as I admire your fortune-telling powers, Esmeralda, my dear child, I think I will just go ahead and do it anyway, if it's all the same to you.'

Esmeralda shook her head. 'Don't say you weren't warned!'

'Pah!' snorted Percy. 'Roamany magic! Fortune-telling! It's all nothing but hedgerow tricks!'

Trundle turned to Esmeralda. 'What do you think is going to happen?' he whispered.

'I don't know,' Esmeralda whispered back. 'It's just a feeling. But I think we should stand well back.'

The two friends moved away from the altar. Percy stood over the slot. He aimed the trembling sword point down and thrust it deep into the stone.

Things started happening almost immediately.

Blue lightning flickered along the blade of the sword. Crackling and spitting, it travelled quickly up Percy's arms and spread out over his body till he was surrounded in a halo of hissing blue lightning.

'That's more like it!' Percy said, lifting his snout to the roof. 'Crowns of the Badger Lords, awake!' he called.

The blue lightning sent crackling tendrils out to the six crowns. 'Ooh! It tickles!' said Percy. But then he tried to let go of the sword. His expression changed as he heaved and strained, trying desperately to get his hands free. The sword wouldn't release him. His hands were stuck fast to the hilt.

'Uh-oh! Here goes!' said Esmeralda. 'You might not want to look, Trundle!'

But what happened next happened so quickly, that Trundle didn't even have time to look away.

Dread swept over Percy's face. He let out a croaking gasp as the blue lightning played all over his body. And then, as Trundle watched in growing horror, the Herald Persuivant began rapidly to age, as though all those hundreds and hundreds of years of life he had stolen with the Vile Rune were catching up with him in a few seconds.

His prickles went white and his face grew sunken and wrinkled. Trundle could see his body shrinking under his robes, until he seemed no more than skin and bones. And then, almost before Trundle could catch his breath, Percy's robes crumpled empty to the white stone, and nothing was left of Grinder Prickleback but fine grey dust.

'Well, that certainly served him right!' Esmeralda said heartlessly. 'He can't say I didn't warn him.'

'I suppose not,' gulped Trundle, feeling a little queasy – seeing Percy turn to powder had been really rather unpleasant. 'What do we do now?'

'I think we should get out of here!' said Esmeralda. 'I've got a feeling something big is about to happen!'

But before they were able to take even a single step towards the doorway, something big *did* happen.

The whole of the chamber shook and trembled. The ground vibrated under Trundle and Esmeralda's feet. Cracks ran up the walls. Dust and shards of stone rained down. And then, with a splintering and splitting and booming sound, the domed roof broke open, peeling back like the skin of an orange to reveal the bright, sunlit sky.

And while Trundle and Esmeralda were still blinking in the dazzling light, creepers and tendrils and roots came snaking out of the cracks in the walls of the chamber, sprouting leaves and buds, creeping across the floor so that they had to dance about not to get tangled up in them.

'The crowns are waking up all right!' shouted Esmeralda. 'Keep your head down, Trundle! Things are getting interesting!'

She had hardly finished speaking when thick black clouds came rolling in over the blue sky, throwing down deep dark shadows. And from the belly of the clouds, a sudden storm of hail came rattling down through the open dome of the chamber, bouncing up cold and hard off the stone altar.

Trundle gazed up in alarm as a blazing flurry of shooting stars went hurtling across the darkened sky, their fiery tails streaming out behind.

And as the light from the stars illuminated the cave, the blue lightning began to spark between the crowns. Arcs of blue fire crackled from one to the other, moving faster and faster, until the crowns could hardly be seen.

And as the tornado of blue energy swirled, so things began to be sucked in; small things at first, pebbles and stones from the floor and walls, whipping through the air and crashing into the whirl in a shower of sparks.

Trundle felt himself being tugged towards the heart of the tornado. Things were zipping past his ears. He clutched hold of Esmeralda to save himself from being pulled in. She was clinging grimly to a thick root, her clothes cracking and flapping in the cyclone of rushing air.

'Hang on!' Trundle yelled to Esmeralda above the noise. 'We mustn't get sucked in!'

'I know!' hollered Esmeralda. 'Oh, heck – I'm slipping, *Tru-un*!' With a frantic yelp, Esmeralda lost grip on the root and she and Trundle went sailing off through the air like a couple of leaves in an autumn gale.

Trundle winced, expecting to be blasted to little pieces as he hit the blue whirlwind. But even as the two of them went flying through the air, the whirl of spitting lightning slowed and turned all to gold.

And it was warm! Trundle felt himself buoyed up on updraughts of warm golden air. He clung to Esmeralda's hand as the two of them went floating up and up and up, through the broken roof of the cavern, flying in the air like thistledown, surrounded by soft billowing clouds of golden light.

'What's going on?' Trundle gasped, staring down between his feet as the barren rocky landscape of Sunsett fell away beneath them.

'Beats me, Trun,' laughed Esmeralda. 'But it's fun, isn't it?'

Trundle began to laugh, as though there was something in the clouds of golden light that took all his cares and worries away.

And as they rose into the sky, so the dark clouds dissolved and everything was once more bathed in the brilliant light of the sleepless sun.

'Whee-ooo!' squealed Esmeralda, turning summersaults in the air. 'I like it!'

'Me too!' yelled Trundle, rolling over and over and laughing out loud.

At last they stopped rising into the air, and they found the golden clouds under their feet were solid enough for them to stand up. And as they stood there, hand in hand, they saw a marvellous sight.

Nightreef was coming apart in front of their eyes, the whole barrier of rocks and rubble breaking into fragments that drifted off like great dark windgalleons. And beyond the shards of Nightreef, they saw all the vast scattered islands of the Sundered Lands being bathed in a sudden sunlight.

'Gosh!' breathed Esmeralda. 'Isn't that spectacular!'

But more was to come. As Trundle gazed in wide-eyed amazement, he saw the islands of the Sundered Lands begin to move together.

'The legends were right!' he gasped. 'The Sundered Lands are being reunited!'

'It's going to be the World again!' said Esmeralda. She squeezed Trundle's hand. 'And we did it!'

As they hung there in the golden air, the thousands of islands came gently together, bumping and nudging up against one another, melting into one, merging and joining, forming a gigantic ball under their floating feet. And Trundle was quite certain he heard the sound of voices laughing and cheering from the newly reunited sphere.

And then the golden light began to swirl and to

change and to form shapes in the sky. Shapes that were

as huge as mountains – huger than the hugest

mountains Trundle could ever imagine. And the shapes

were the shapes of six Badger Lords, old and wise and venerable, like golden clouds smiling down upon the new-made globe of the world.

Trundle heard a voice in his ear. 'Well done, Lamplighter! Well done, Princess in Darkness! Well done, indeed!'

And with that, a breeze caught the six golden Badger Lords, and they lost their shapes and dissolved away like mist.

Trundle and Esmeralda felt themselves floating like feathers down to the ground. But it wasn't the island of Sunsett that their feet landed on. It wasn't an island at all. It was just one small part of the huge ball that was the world.

'Well,' breathed Esmeralda, 'we did it, Trun!' She slapped him heartily on the back. 'You became a hero, whether you liked it or not!'

'I do believe I did,' said Trundle, looking

around himself. The chamber of the stone altar was nowhere to be seen. Neither was the cliff with the temple carved into its face. And neither was *The Thief in the Night*. They were in a sandy valley – but not too far off, at the end of the valley, they could see palm trees waving.

'Where's our skyboat?' Trundle wondered.

'Who needs it?' laughed Esmeralda. 'We can *walk* to wherever we like!'

'Then let's get going,' said Trundle, gazing towards the distant trees. 'Where should we go first?'

'That's up to you, Trundle, my lad!' said Esmeralda, slipping her arm into his. 'Where would you like to go?'

Trundle grinned at her. 'Anywhere but Shiverstones!' he said.

'That's fine with me!'

And so saying, the two friends went marching off down the valley. In his heart of hearts, all that Trundle Boldoak wanted was for their adventures to go on for ever!

For competitions, downloads and games, visit:

www.sunderedlands.co.uk

The SPINDLEWOOD TALES

From the creator of *Something Wickedly Weird* comes Pip and friends! Join them on their adventures in the great walled city of Hangman's Hollow ...

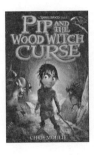

'A riveting yarn that is thrilling and haunting by turns.'

Junior Magazine

CHRIS MOULD

Also available as an ebook

www.chrismouldink.com
www.hodderchildrens.co.uk

Hodder Children's Books